HIGH NOON

CLASSIC TALES OF THE WILD WEST

**HOPALONG CASSIDY
THE CISCO KID
STAGECOACH
DESTRY RIDES AGAIN
WESTERN UNION
THE VIRGINIAN**

BY

VARIOUS AUTHORS

British Library Cataloguing-in-Publication Data
A catalogue record for this book is available from the
British Library

CONTENTS

HOPALONG CASSIDY

CLARENCE E. MULFORD

The town lay sprawled over half a square mile of alkali plain, its main street depressing in its width, for those who were responsible for its inception had worked with a generosity born of the knowledge that they had at their immediate and unchallenged disposal the broad lands of Texas and New Mexico on which to assemble a grand total of twenty buildings, four of which were of wood. As this material was scarce, and had to be brought from where the waters of the Gulf lapped against the flat coast, the last-mentioned buildings were a matter of local pride, as indicating the progressiveness of their owners. These creations of hammer and saw were of one storey, crude and unpainted; their cheap weather sheathing, warped and shrunken by the pitiless sun, curled back on itself and allowed unrestricted entrance to alkali dust and air. The other shacks were of adobe, and reposed in that magnificent squalor dear to their owners, Indians and 'Greasers'.

It was an incident of the Cattle Trail, that most unique and stupendous of all modern migrations, and its founders must have been inspired with a malicious desire to perpetrate a crime against geography, or else they revelled in a perverse cussedness, for within a mile on every side lay broad prairies, and two miles to the east flowed the indolent waters of the Rio Pecos itself. The distance separating the town from the river was excusable, for at certain seasons of the year the placid stream swelled mightily and swept down in a broad expanse of turbulent yellow flood.

Buckskin was a town of one hundred inhabitants, located in the valley of the Rio Pecos fifty miles south of the Texas–New Mexico line. The census claimed two hundred, but it was a well-known fact that it was exaggerated. One instance of this is shown at the name of Tom Flynn. Those who once knew Tom Flynn, alias Johnny Redmond, alias Bill Sweeney, alias Chuck Mullen, by all four names, could find them in the census list. Furthermore, he had been shot and killed in the March of the year preceding the census, and now occupied a grave in the young but flourishing cemetery. Perry's Bend, twenty miles up the river, was cognisant of this and other facts, and, laughing in open derision at the padded list, claimed to be the better town in all ways, including marksmanship.

One year before this tale opens, Buck Peters, an example

for the more recent Billy the Kid, had paid Perry's Bend a short but busy visit. He had ridden in at the north end of Main street and out at the south. As he came in he was fired at by a group of ugly cowboys from a ranch known as the C 80. He was hit twice, but he unlimbered his artillery, and before his horse had carried him, half dead, out on the prairie, he had killed one of the group. Several citizens had joined the cowboys and added their bullets against Buck. The deceased had been the best bartender in the country, and the rage of the suffering citizens can well be imagined. They swore vengeance on Buck, his ranch and his stamping ground.

The difference between Buck and Billy the Kid is that the former never shot a man who was not trying to shoot him, or who had not been warned by some action against Buck that would call for it. He minded his own business, never picked a quarrel and was quiet and pacific up to a certain point. After that had been passed he became like a raging cyclone in a tenement house, and storm-cellars were much in demand.

'Fanning' is the name of a certain style of gunplay and was universal among the bad men of the West. While Buck was not a bad man, he had to rub elbows with them frequently, and he believed that the sauce for the goose was the sauce for the gander. So he had removed the trigger of his revolver and worked the hammer with the thumb of the 'gun hand' or the thumb of the unencumbered hand. The speed thus acquired was greater than that of the more modern double-action weapon. Six shots in three seconds was his average speed when that number was required, and when it is thoroughly understood that at least five of them found their intended billets it is not difficult to realize that fanning was an operation of danger when Buck was doing it.

He was a good rider, as all cowboys are, and was not afraid of anything that lived. At one time he and his chums, Red Connors and Hopalong Cassidy, had successfully routed a band of fifteen Apaches who wanted their scalps. Of these, twelve never hunted scalps again, nor anything else on this earth, and the other three returned to their tribe with the report that three evil spirits had chased them with 'wheel guns' (cannons).

So now, since his visit to Perry's Bend, the rivalry of the two towns had turned to hatred and an alert and eager readiness to increase the inhabitants of each other's graveyard. A state of war existed, which for a time resulted in nothing worse than acrimonious suggestions. But the time came when the score was settled to the satisfaction of one side, at least.

Four ranches were also concerned in the trouble. Buckskin was surrounded by two, the Bar 20 and the Three Triangle. Perry's Bend was the common point for the C 80 and the

Double Arrow. Each of the two ranch contingents accepted the feud as a matter of course, and as a matter of course took sides with their respective towns. As no better class of fighters ever lived, the trouble assumed Homeric proportions and insured a danger zone well worth watching.

Bar 20's northern line was C 80's southern one, and Skinny Thompson took his turn at outriding one morning after the season's round-up. He was to follow the boundary and turn back stray cattle. When he had covered the greater part of his journey he saw Shorty Jones riding toward him on a course parallel to his own and about long revolver range away. Shorty and he had 'crossed trails' the year before and the best of feelings did not exist between them.

Shorty stopped and stared at Skinny, who did likewise at Shorty. Shorty turned his mount around and applied the spurs, thereby causing his indignant horse to raise both heels at Skinny. The latter took it all in gravely and, as Shorty faced him again, placed his left thumb to his nose, wiggling his fingers suggestively. Shorty took no apparent notice of this, but began to shout:

"Yu wants to keep yore busted-down cows on yore own side. They was all over us day afore yisterday. I'm goin' to salt any more what comes over, and don't yu fergit it, neither."

Thompson wigwagged with his fingers again and shouted in reply: "Yu c'n salt all yu wants to, but if I ketch yu adoin' it yu won't have to work no more. An' I kin say right here thet they's more C 80 cows over here than they's Bar 20's over there."

Shorty reached for his revolver and yelled, "Yore a liar!"

Among the cowboys in particular and the Westerners in general at that time, the three suicidal terms, unless one was an expert in drawing quick and shooting straight with one movement, were the words 'liar', 'coward' and 'thief'. Any man who was called one of these in earnest, and he was the judge, was expected to shoot if he could and save his life, for the words were seldom used without a gun coming with them. The movement of Shorty's hand toward his belt before the appellation reached him was enough for Skinny, who let go at long range – and missed.

The two reports were as one. Both urged their horses nearer and fired again. This time Skinny's sombrero gave a sharp jerk and a hole appeared in the crown. The third shot of Skinny's sent the horse of the other to its knees and then over on its side. Shorty very promptly crawled behind it and, as he did so, Skinny began a wide circle, firing at intervals as Shorty's smoke cleared away.

Shorty had the best position for defence, as he was in a shallow coulée, but he knew that he could not leave it until his opponent had either grown tired of the affair or had used up his ammunition. Skinny knew it, too. Skinny also knew that he could get back to the ranch-house and lay in a supply of food and ammunition and return before Shorty could cover the twelve miles he had to go on foot.

Finally, Thompson began to head for home. He had carried the matter as far as he could without it being murder. Too much time had elapsed now, and, besides, it was before breakfast and he was hungry. He would go away and settle the score at some time when they would be on equal terms.

He rode along the line for a mile and chanced to look back. Two C 80 punchers were riding after him, and as they saw him turn and discover them they fired at him and yelled. He rode on for some distance and cautiously drew his rifle out of its long holster at his right leg. Suddenly he turned around in the saddle and fired twice. One of his pursuers fell forward on the neck of his horse, and his comrade turned to help him. Thompson wigwagged again and rode on, reaching the ranch as the others were finishing their breakfast.

At the table Red Connors remarked that the tardy one had a hole in his sombrero, and asked its owner how and where he had received it.

"Had a argument with C 80 out 'n th' line."

"Go 'way! Ventilate enny?"

"One."

"Good boy, sonny! Hey, Hopalong, Skinny perforated C 80 this mawnin'!"

Hopalong Cassidy was struggling with a mouthful of beef. He turned his eyes toward Red without ceasing, and grinning as well as he could under the circumstances managed to grunt out "Gu –", which was as near to "Good" as the beef would allow.

Lanky Smith now chimed in as he repeatedly stuck his knife into a reluctant boiled potato, "How'd yu do it, Skinny?"

"Bet he sneaked up on him," joshed Buck Peters; "did yu ask his pardin, Skinny?"

"Ask nothin'," remarked Red, "he jest nachurly walks up to C 80 an' sez, 'Kin I have the pleasure of ventilatin' yu?' an' C 80 he sez, 'If yu do it easy like,' sez he. Didn't he, Thompson?"

"They'll be some ventilatin' under th' table if yu fellows don't lemme alone; I'm hungry," complained Skinny.

"Say, Hopalong, I bets yu I kin clean up C 80 all by my lonesome," announced Buck, winking at Red.

"Yah! Yu once tried to clean up the Bend, Buckie, an' if Pete an' Billy hadn't afound yu when they come by Eagle Pass that night yu wouldn't be here eatin' beef by th' pound," glancing at the hard-working Hopalong. "It was plum' lucky fer yu that they was acourtin' that time, wasn't it, Hopalong?" suddenly asked Red. Hopalong nearly strangled in his efforts to speak. He gave it up and nodded his head.

"Why can't yu git it straight, Connors? I wasn't doin' no courtin', it was Pete. I runned into him on th' other side o' th' pass. I'd look fine acourtin', wouldn't I?" asked the downtrodden Williams.

Pete Wilson skilfully flipped a potato into that worthy's coffee, spilling the beverage of the questionable name over a large expanse of blue flannel shirt.

"Yu's all right, yu are. Why, when I meets yu, yu was lost in th' arms of yore ladylove. All I could see was yore feet. Go an' git tangled up with a two-hundred-and-forty-pound half-breed squaw an' then try to lay it onter me! When I proposed drownin' yore troubles over at Cowan's, yu went an' got mad over what yu called th' insinooation. An' yu shore didn't look any too blamed fine, neither."

"All th' same," volunteered Thompson, who had taken the edge from his appetite, "we better go over an' pay C 80 a call. I don't like what Shorty said about saltin' our cattle. He'll shore do it, unless I camps on th' line, which same I hain't hankerin' after."

"Oh, he wouldn't stop th' cows that way, Skinny; he was only afoolin'," exclaimed Connors meekly.

"Foolin' yore gran'mother! That there bunch'll do anything if we wasn't lookin'," hotly replied Skinny.

"That's shore nuff gospel, Thomp. They's sore fer mor'n one thing. They got aplenty when Buck went on th' warpath, an' they's hankerin' to git square," remarked Johnny Nelson, stealing the pie, a rare treat, of his neighbour when that unfortunate individual was not looking. He had it half-way to his mouth when its former owner, Jimmy Price, a boy of eighteen, turned his head and saw it going.

"Hi-yi! Yu clay-bank coyete, drap that pie! Did yu ever see such a son-of-a-gun fer pie?" he plaintively asked Red Connors, as he grabbed a mighty handful of apples and crust. "Pie'll kill yu some day, yu bob-tailed jack! I had an uncle that died once. He et too much pie an' he went an' turned green, an' so'll yu if yu don't let it alone."

"Yu ought'r seed th' pie Johnny had down in Eagle Flat," murmured Lanky Smith reminiscently. "She had feet that'd stop a stam*pede*. Johnny was shore loco about her. Swore she was the finest blossom that ever growed." Here he choked and tears of laughter coursed down his weatherbeaten face as he pictured her. "She was a dainty Greaser, about fifteen han's high an' about sixteen han's around. Johnny used to chalk off when he hugged her, usen't yu, Johnny? One night when he had got purty well around on th' second lap he run inter a Greaser jest startin' out on his fust. They hain't caught that Mexican yet."

Nelson was pelted with everything in sight. He slowly wiped off the pie crust and bread and potatoes.

"Anybody'd think I was a busted grub wagon," he

grumbled. When he had fished the last piece of beef out of his ear he went out and offered to stand treat. As the round-up was over, they slid into their saddles and raced for Cowan's saloon at Buckskin.

THE CISCO KID

O. HENRY

The Cisco Kid had killed six men in more or less fair scrimmages, had murdered twice as many (mostly Mexicans) and had winged a larger number whom he modestly forbore to count. Therefore a woman loved him.

The Kid was twenty-five, looked twenty; and a careful insurance company would have estimated the probable time of his demise at, say, twenty-six. His habitat was anywhere between the Frio and the Rio Grande. He killed for the love of it – because he was quick-tempered – to avoid arrest – for his own amusement – any reason that came to his mind would suffice. He had escaped capture because he could shoot five-sixths of a second sooner than any sheriff or ranger in the service, and because he rode a speckled roan horse that knew every cow-path in the mesquite and pear thickets from San Antonio to Matamoras.

Tonia Perez, the girl who loved the Cisco Kid, was half Carmen, half Madonna, and the rest – oh, yes, a woman who is half Carmen and half Madonna can always be something more – the rest, let us say, was humming-bird. She lived in a grass-roofed *jacal* near a little Mexican settlement at the Lone Wolf Crossing of the Frio. With her lived a father or grandfather, a lineal Aztec, somewhat less than a thousand years old, who herded a hundred goats and lived in a continuous drunken dream from drinking *mescal*. Back of the *jacal* a tremendous forest of bristling pear, twenty feet high at its worst, crowded almost to its door. It was along the bewildering maze of this spinous thicket that the speckled roan would bring the Kid to see his girl. And once, clinging like a lizard to the ridge-pole, high up under the peaked grass roof, he had heard Tonia, with her Madonna face and Carmen beauty and humming-bird soul, parley with the sheriff's posse, denying knowledge of her man in her soft *mélange* of Spanish and English.

One day the adjutant-general of the State, who is, *ex officio*, commander of the ranger forces, wrote some sarcastic lines to Captain Duval of Company X, stationed at Laredo, relative to the serene and undisturbed existence led by murderers and desperadoes in the said captain's territory.

The captain turned the colour of brick dust under his tan, and forwarded the letter, after adding a few comments, per ranger Private Bill Adamson, to ranger Lieutenant Sandridge, camped at a waterhole on the Nueces with a squad of five men in preservation of law and order.

Lieutenant Sandridge turned a beautiful *couleur de rose* through his ordinary strawberry complexion, tucked the letter in his hip pocket and chewed off the ends of his gamboge moustache.

The next morning he saddled his horse and rode alone to the Mexican settlement at the Lone Wolf Crossing of the Frio, twenty miles away.

Six feet two, blond as a Viking, quiet as a deacon, dangerous as a machine-gun, Sandridge moved among the *jacales*, patiently seeking news of the Cisco Kid.

Far more than the law, the Mexicans dreaded the cold and certain vengeance of the lone rider that the ranger sought. It had been one of the Kid's pastimes to shoot Mexicans 'to see them kick': if he demanded from them moribund Terpsichorean feats, simply that he might be entertained, what terrible and extreme penalties would be certain to follow should they anger him! One and all they lounged with upturned palms and shrugging shoulders, filling the air with '*quien sabes*' and denials of the Kid's acquaintance.

But there was a man named Fink who kept a store at the Crossing – a man of many nationalities, tongues, interests and ways of thinking.

"No use to ask them Mexicans," he said to Sandridge. "They're afraid to tell. This *hombre* they call the Kid – Goodall is his name, ain't it? – he's been in my store once or twice. I have an idea you might run across him at – but I guess I don't keer to say, myself. I'm two seconds later in pulling a gun than I used to be, and the difference is worth thinking about. But this Kid's got a half-Mexican girl at the Crossing that he comes to see. She lives in that *jacal* a hundred yards down the arroyo at the edge of the pear. Maybe she – no, I don't suppose she would, but that *jacal* would be a good place to watch, anyway."

Sandridge rode down to the *jacal* of Perez. The sun was low, and the broad shade of the great pear thicket already covered the grass-thatched hut. The goats were enclosed for the night in a brush corral near by. A few kids walked the top of it, nibbling the chaparral leaves. The old Mexican lay upon a blanket on the grass, already in a stupor from his *mescal*, and dreaming, perhaps, of the nights when he and Pizarro touched glasses to their New World fortunes – so old his wrinkled face seemed to proclaim him to be. And in the door of the *jacal* stood Tonia. And Lieutenant Sandridge sat in his saddle staring at her like a gannet agape at a sailorman.

The Cisco Kid was a vain person, as all eminent and successful assassins are, and his bosom would have been ruffled had he known that at a simple exchange of glances two persons, in whose minds he had been looming large, suddenly abandoned (at least for the time) all thought of him.

Never before had Tonia seen such a man as this. He seemed to be made of sunshine and blood-red tissue and clear weather. He seemed to illuminate the shadow of the pear when he smiled, as though the sun were rising again. The men she had known had been small and dark. Even the kid, in spite of his achievements, was a stripling no larger than herself, with black, straight hair and a cold, marble face that chilled the noonday.

As for Tonia, though she sends description to the poorhouse, let her make a millionaire of your fancy. Her blue-black hair, smoothly divided in the middle and bound close to her head, and her large eyes full of the Latin melancholy, gave her the Madonna touch. Her motions and air spoke of the concealed fire and the desire to charm that she had inherited from the *gitanas* of the Basque province. As for the humming-bird part of her, that dwelt in her heart; you could not perceive it unless her bright red skirt and dark blue blouse gave you a symbolic hint of the vagarious bird.

The newly lighted sun-god asked for a drink of water. Tonia brought it from the red jar hanging under the brush shelter. Sandridge considered it necessary to dismount so as to lessen the trouble of her ministrations.

I play no spy; nor do I assume to master the thoughts of any human heart; but I assert, by the chronicler's right, that before a quarter of an hour had sped, Sandridge was teaching her how to plait a six-strand rawhide stake-rope, and Tonia had explained to him that were it not for her little English book that the peripatetic *padre* had given her and the little crippled *chivo*, that she fed from a bottle, she would be very, very lonely indeed.

Which leads to a suspicion that the Kid's fences needed repairing, and that the adjutant-general's sarcasm had fallen upon unproductive soil.

In his camp by the waterhole Lieutenant Sandridge announced and reiterated his intention of either causing the Cisco Kid to nibble the black loam of the Frio country prairies or of haling him before a judge and jury. That sounded businesslike. Twice a week he rode over to the Lone Wolf Crossing of the Frio, and directed Tonia's slim, slightly lemon-tinted fingers among the intricacies of the slowly growing lariata. A six-strand plait is hard to learn and easy to teach.

The ranger knew that he might find the Kid there at any visit. He kept his armament ready, and had a frequent eye for the pear thicket at the rear of the *jacal*. Thus he might bring down the kite and the humming-bird with one stone.

While the sunny-haired ornithologist was pursuing his studies the Cisco Kid was also attending to his professional duties. He moodily shot up a saloon in a small cow village on Quintana Creek, killed the town marshal (plugging him neatly in the centre of his tin badge) and then rode away, morose and unsatisfied. No true artist is uplifted by shooting an aged man carrying an old-style .38 bulldog.

On his way the Kid suddenly experienced the yearning that all men feel when wrongdoing loses its keen edge of delight. He yearned for the woman he loved to reassure him that she was his in spite of it. He wanted her to call his bloodthirstiness bravery and his cruelty devotion. He wanted Tonia to bring him water from the red jar under the brush shelter, and tell him how the *chivo* was thriving on the bottle.

The Kid turned the speckled roan's head up the ten-mile pear flat that stretches along the Arroyo Hondo until it ends at the Lone Wolf Crossing of the Frio. The roan whickered, for he had a sense of locality and direction equal to that of a belt-line street-car horse; and he knew he would soon be nibbling the rich mesquite grass at the end of a forty-foot stake-rope while Ulysses rested his head in Circe's straw-roofed hut.

More weird and lonesome than the journey of an Amazonian explorer is the ride of one through a Texas pear flat. With dismal monotony and startling variety the uncanny and multiform shapes of the cacti lift their twisted trunks, and fat, bristly hands to encumber the way. The demon plant, appearing to live without soil or rain, seems to taunt the parched traveller with its lush grey greenness. It warps itself a thousand times about what look to be open and inviting paths, only to lure the rider into blind and impassable spine-defended 'bottoms of the bad', leaving him to retreat, if he can, with the points of the compass whirling in his head.

To be lost in the pear is to die almost the death of the thief on the cross, pierced by nails and with grotesque shapes of all the fiends hovering about.

But it was not so with the Kid and his mount. Winding, twisting, circling, tracing the most fantastic and bewildering trail ever picked out, the good roan lessened the distance to the Lone Wolf Crossing with every coil and turn that he made.

While they fared the Kid sang. He knew but one tune and sang it, as he knew but one code and lived it and but one girl and loved her. He was a single-minded man of conventional ideas. He had a voice like a coyote with bronchitis, but whenever he chose to sing his song he sang it. It was a conventional song of the camps and trail, running at its beginning as near as may be to these words:

Don't you monkey with my Lulu girl
Or I'll tell you what I'll do —

and so on. The roan was inured to it, and did not mind.

But even the poorest singer will, after a certain time, gain his own consent to refrain from contributing to the world's noises. So the Kid, by the time he was within a mile or two of Tonia's *jacal*, had reluctantly allowed his song to die away – not because his vocal performance had become less charming to his own ears, but because his laryngeal muscles were aweary.

As though he were in a circus ring the speckled roan wheeled and danced through the labyrinth of pear until at length his rider knew by certain landmarks that the Lone Wolf Crossing was close at hand. Then, where the pear was thinner, he caught sight of the grass roof of the *jacal* and the hackberry tree on the edge of the arroyo. A few yards farther the Kid stopped the roan and gazed intently through the prickly openings. Then he dismounted, dropped the roan's reins, and proceeded on foot, stooping and silent, like an Indian. The roan, knowing his part, stood still, making no sound.

The Kid crept noiselessly to the very edge of the pear thicket and reconnoitered between the leaves of a clump of cactus.

Ten yards from his hiding place, in the shade of the

jacal, sat his Tonia calmly plaiting a rawhide lariat. So far she might surely escape condemnation; women have been known, from time to time, to engage in more mischievous occupations. But if all must be told, there is to be added that her head reposed against the broad and comfortable chest of a tall red-and-yellow man, and that his arm was about her, guiding her nimble small fingers that required so many lessons at the intricate six-strand plait.

Sandridge glanced quickly at the dark mass of pear when he heard a slight squeaking sound that was not altogether unfamiliar. A gun scabbard will make that sound when one grasps the handle of a six-shooter suddenly. But the sound was not repeated; and Tonia's fingers needed close attention.

And then, in the shadow of death, they began to talk of their love; and in the still July afternoon every word they uttered reached the ears of the Kid.

"Remember, then," said Tonia, "you must not come again until I send for you. Soon he will be here. A *vaquero* at the *tienda* said today he saw him on the Guadalupe three days ago. When he is that near he always comes. If he comes and finds you here he will kill you. So, for my sake, you must come no more until I send you the word."

"All right," said the ranger. "And then what?"

"And then," said the girl, "you must bring your men here and kill him. If not, he will kill you."

"He ain't a man to surrender, that's sure," said Sandridge. "It's kill or be killed for the officer that goes up against Mr Cisco Kid."

"He must die," said the girl. "Otherwise there will not be any peace in the world for thee and me. He has killed many. Let him so die. Bring your men, and give him no chance to escape."

"You used to think right much of him," said Sandridge.

Tonia dropped the lariat, twisted herself around and curved a lemon-tinted arm over the ranger's shoulder.

"But then," she murmured in liquid Spanish, "I had not beheld thee, thou great, red mountain of a man! And thou art kind and good, as well as strong. Could one choose him, knowing thee? Let him die; for then I will not be filled with fear by day and night lest he hurt thee or me."

"How can I know when he comes?" asked Sandridge.

"When he comes," said Tonia, "he remains two days, sometimes three. Gregorio, the small son of old Luisa, the *lavandera*, has a swift pony. I will write a letter to thee and send it by him, saying how it will be best to come upon him. By Gregorio will the letter come. And bring many men with thee, and have much care, oh, dear red one, for the rattlesnake is not quicker to strike than is 'El Chivato', as they call him, to send a ball from his *pistola*."

"The Kid's handy with his gun, sure enough," admitted

Sandridge, "but when I come for him I shall come alone. I'll get him by myself or not at all. The Cap wrote one or two things to me that make me want to do the trick without any help. You let me know when Mr Kid arrives, and I'll do the rest."

"I will send you the message by the boy Gregorio," said the girl. "I knew you were braver than that small slayer of men who never smiles. How could I ever have thought I cared for him?"

It was time for the ranger to ride back to his camp on the waterhole. Before he mounted his horse he raised the slight form of Tonia with one arm high from the earth for a parting salute. The drowsy stillness of the torpid summer air still lay thick upon the dreaming afternoon. The smoke from the fire in the *jacal*, where the *frijoles* blubbered in the iron pot, rose straight as a plumb-line above the clay-daubed chimney. No sound or movement disturbed the serenity of the dense pear thicket ten yards away.

When the form of Sandridge had disappeared, loping his big dun down the steep banks of the Frio crossing, the Kid crept back to his own horse, mounted him, and rode back along the tortuous trail he had come.

But not far. He stopped and waited in the silent depths of the pear until half an hour had passed. And then Tonia heard the high, untrue notes of his unmusical singing coming nearer and nearer; and she ran to the edge of the pear to meet him.

The Kid seldom smiled; but he smiled and waved his hat when he saw her. He dismounted, and his girl sprang into his arms. The Kid looked at her fondly. His thick, black hair clung to his head like a wrinkled mat. The meeting brought a slight ripple of some undercurrent of feeling to his smooth, dark face that was usually as motionless as a clay mask.

"How's my girl?" he asked, holding her close.

"Sick of waiting so long for you, dear one," she answered. "My eyes are dim with always gazing into that devil's pincushion through which you come. And I can see into it such a little way, too. But you are here, beloved one, and I will not scold. *Que mal muchacho!* not to come to see your *alma* more often. Go in and rest, and let me water your horse and stake him with the long rope. There is cool water in the jar for you."

The Kid kissed her affectionately.

"Not if the court knows itself do I let a lady stake my horse for me," said he. "But if you'll run in, *chica*, and throw a pot of coffee together while I attend to the *caballo*, I'll be a good deal obliged."

Besides his marksmanship the Kid had another attribute for which he admired himself greatly. He was *muy caballero*, as the Mexicans express it, where the ladies were concerned.

For them he had always gentle words and consideration. He could not have spoken a harsh word to a woman. He might ruthlessly slay their husbands and brothers, but he could not have laid the weight of a finger in anger upon a woman. Wherefore many of that interesting division of humanity who had come under the spell of his politeness declared their disbelief in the stories circulated about Mr Kid. One shouldn't believe everything one heard, they said. When confronted by their indignant menfolk with proof of the *caballero's* deeds of infamy, they said maybe he had been driven to it, and that he knew how to treat a lady, anyhow.

Considering this extremely courteous idiosyncrasy of the Kid and the pride that he took in it, one can perceive that the solution of the problem that was presented to him by what he saw and heard from his hiding place in the pear that afternoon (at least as to one of the actors) must have been obscured by difficulties. And yet one could not think of the Kid overlooking little matters of that kind.

At the end of the short twilight they gathered around a supper of *frijoles*, goat steaks, canned peaches and coffee, by the light of a lantern in the *jacal*. Afterward, the ancestor, his flock corralled, smoked a cigarette and became a mummy in a grey blanket. Tonia washed the few dishes while the Kid dried them with the flour-sacking towel. Her eyes shone; she chatted volubly of the inconsequent happenings of her small world since the Kid's last visit; it was as all his other home-comings had been.

Then outside Tonia swung in a grass hammock with her guitar and sang sad *canciones de amor*.

"Do you love me just the same, old girl?" asked the Kid, hunting for his cigarette papers.

"Always the same, little one," said Tonia, her dark eyes lingering upon him.

"I must go over to Fink's," said the Kid, rising, "for some tobacco. I thought I had another sack in my coat. I'll be back in a quarter of an hour."

"Hasten," said Tonia, "and tell me – how long shall I call you my own this time? Will you be gone again tomorrow, leaving me to grieve, or will you be longer with your Tonia?"

"Oh, I might stay two or three days this trip," said the Kid, yawning. "I've been on the dodge for a month, and I'd like to rest up."

He was gone half an hour for his tobacco. When he returned Tonia was still lying in the hammock.

"It's funny," said the Kid, "how I feel. I feel like there was somebody lying behind every bush and tree waiting to shoot me. I never had mullygrubs like them before. Maybe it's one of them presumptions. I've got half a notion to light out in the morning before day. The Guadalupe country is burning up about that old Dutchman I plugged down there."

"You are not afraid – no one could make my brave little one fear."

"Well, I haven't been usually regarded as a jack-rabbit when it comes to scrapping; but I don't want a posse smoking me out when I'm in your *jacal*. Somebody might get hurt that oughtn't to."

"Remain with your Tonia; no one will find you here."

The Kid looked keenly into the shadows up and down the arroyo and toward the dim lights of the Mexican village.

"I'll see how it looks later on," was his decision.

At midnight a horseman rode into the rangers' camp, blazing his way by noisy 'halloes' to indicate a pacific mission. Sandridge and one or two others turned out to investigate the row. The rider announced himself to be Domingo Sales, from the Lone Wolf Crossing. He bore a letter for Señor Sandridge. Old Luisa, the *lavandera*, had persuaded him to bring it, he said, her son Gregorio being too ill of a fever to ride.

Sandridge lighted the camp lantern and read the letter. These were its words:

Dear One: He has come. Hardly had you ridden away when he came out of the pear. When he first talked he said he would stay three days or more. Then as it grew later he was like a wolf or a fox, and walked about without rest, looking and listening. Soon he said he must leave before daylight when it is dark and stillest. And then he seemed to suspect that I be not true to him. He looked at me so strange that I am frightened. I swear to him that I love him, his own Tonia. Last of all he said I must prove to him I am true. He thinks that even now men are waiting to kill him as he rides from my house. To escape he says he will dress in my clothes, my red skirt and the blue waist I wear and the brown mantilla over the head, and thus ride away. But before that he says that I must put on his clothes, his *pantalones* and *camisa* and hat, and ride away on his horse from the *jacal* as far as the big road beyond the crossing and back again. This before he goes, so he can tell if I am true and if men are hidden to shoot him. It is a terrible thing. An hour before daybreak this is to be. Come, my dear one, and kill this man and take me for your Tonia. Do not try to take hold of him alive, but kill him quickly. Knowing all, you should do that. You must come long before the time and hide yourself in the little shed near the *jacal* where the wagon and saddles are kept. It is dark in there. He will wear my red skirt and blue waist and brown mantilla. I send you a hundred kisses. Come surely and shoot quickly and straight.

THINE OWN TONIA.

Sandridge quickly explained to his men the official part of the missive. The rangers protested against his going alone.

"I'll get him easy enough," said the lieutenant. "The girl's got him trapped. And don't even think he'll get the drop on me."

Sandridge saddled his horse and rode to the Lone Wolf Crossing. He tied his big dun in a clump of brush on the arroyo, took his Winchester from its scabbard and carefully approached the Perez *jacal*. There was only the half of a high moon drifted over by ragged, milk-white gulf clouds.

The wagon shed was an excellent place for ambush; and the ranger got inside it safely. In the black shadow of the brush shelter in front of the *jacal* he could see a horse tied and hear him impatiently pawing the hard-trodden earth.

He waited almost an hour before two figures came out of the *jacal*. One, in man's clothes, quickly mounted the horse and galloped past the wagon shed toward the crossing and village. And then the other figure, in skirt, waist, and mantilla over its head, stepped out into the faint moonlight, gazing after the rider. Sandridge thought he would take his chance then before Tonia rode back. He fancied she might not care to see it.

"Throw up your hands," he ordered loudly, stepping out of the wagon shed with his Winchester at his shoulder.

There was a quick turn of the figure, but no movement to obey, so the ranger pumped in the bullets – one – two – three – and then twice more; for you never could be too sure of bringing down the Cisco Kid. There was no danger of missing at ten paces, even in that half moonlight.

The old ancestor, asleep on his blanket, was awakened by the shots. Listening further, he heard a great cry from some man in mortal distress or anguish, and rose up grumbling at the disturbing ways of moderns.

The tall, red ghost of a man burst into the *facal*, reaching one hand, shaking like a *tule* reed, for the lantern hanging on its nail. The other spread a letter on the table.

"Look at this letter, Perez," cried the man. "Who wrote it?"

"Ah, Dios! It is Señor Sandridge," mumbled the old man, approaching. *"Pues, señor,* that letter was written by '*El Chivato*', as he is called – by the man of Tonia. They say he is a bad man; I do not know. While Tonia slept he wrote the letter and sent it by this old hand of mine to Domingo Sales to be brought to you. Is there anything wrong in the letter? I am very old; and I did not know. *Valgame Dios!* It is a very foolish world; and there is nothing in the house to drink – nothing to drink."

Just then all that Sandrige could think of to do was to go outside and throw himself face downward in the dust by the side of his humming-bird, of whom not a feather fluttered. He was not a *caballero* by instinct, and he could not understand the niceties of revenge.

A mile away the rider who had ridden past the wagon shed struck up a harsh, untuneful song, the words of which began:

Don't you monkey with my Lulu girl
Or I'll tell you what I'll do –

STAGECOACH

ERNEST HAYCOX

This was one of those years in the Territory when Apache smoke signals spiralled up from the stony mountain summits and many a ranch cabin lay as a square of blackened ashes on the ground and the departure of a stage from Tonto was the beginning of an adventure that had no certain happy ending.

The stage and its six horses waited in front of Weilner's store on the north side of Tonto's square. Happy Stuart was on the box, the ribbons between his fingers and one foot teetering on the brake. John Strang rode shotgun guard and an escort of ten cavalrymen waited behind the coach, half asleep in their saddles.

At four-thirty in the morning this high air was quite cold, though the sun had begun to flush the sky eastward. A small crowd stood in the square, presenting their final messages to the passengers now entering the coach. There was a girl going down to marry an infantry officer, a whiskey drummer from St Louis, an Englishman all length and bony corners and bearing with him an enormous sporting rifle, a gambler, a solid-shouldered cattleman on his way to New Mexico and a blond young man upon whom both Happy Stuart and the shotgun guard placed a narrow-eyed interest.

This seemed all until the blond man drew back from the coach door; and then a girl known commonly throughout the Territory as Henriette came quietly from the crowd. She was small and quiet, with a touch of paleness in her cheeks and her quite dark eyes lifted at the blond man's unexpected courtesy, showing surprise. There was this moment of delay and then the girl caught up her dress and stepped into the coach.

Men in the crowd were smiling but the blond one turned, his motion like the swift cut of a knife, and his attention covered that group until the smiling quit. He was tall, hollow-flanked and definitely stamped by the guns slung low on his hips. But it wasn't the guns alone; something in his face, so watchful and so smooth, also showed his trade. Afterwards he got into the coach and slammed the door.

Happy Stuart kicked off the brakes and yelled, "Hi!" Tonto's people were calling out their last farewells and the six horses broke into a trot and the stage lunged on its fore and aft springs and rolled from town with dust dripping off its wheels like water, the cavalrymen trotting briskly behind. So they tipped down the long grade, bound on a journey no stage had attempted during the last forty-five days. Out below in the desert's distance stood the relay stations they hoped to reach and pass. Between lay a country swept empty by the quick raids of Geronimo's men.

The Englishman, the gambler and the blond man sat jammed together in the forward seat, riding backward to the course of the stage. The drummer and the cattleman occupied the uncomfortable middle bench; the two women shared the rear seat. The cattleman faced Henriette, his knees almost touching her. He had one arm hooked over the door's window sill to steady himself. A huge gold nugget slid gently back and forth along the watch-chain slung across his wide chest and a chunk of black hair lay below his hat. His eyes considered Henriette, reading something in the girl that caused him to show her a deliberate smile. Henriette dropped her glance to the gloved tips of her fingers, cheeks unstirred.

They were all strangers packed closely together, with nothing in common save a destination. Yet the cattleman's smile and the boldness of his glance were something as audible as speech, noted by everyone except the Englishman, who sat bolt upright with his stony indifference. The army girl, tall and calmly pretty, threw a quick side glance at Henriette and afterwards looked away with a touch of colour. The gambler saw this interchange of glances and showed the cattleman an irritated attention. The whiskey drummer's eyes narrowed a little and some inward cynicism made a faint change on his lips. He removed his hat to show a bald head already beginning to sweat; his cigar smoke turned the coach cloudy and ashes kept dropping on his vest.

The blond man had observed Henriette's glance drop from the cattleman; he tipped his hat well over his face and watched her – not boldly but as though he were puzzled. Once her glance lifted and touched him. But he had been on guard against that and was quick to look away.

The army girl coughed gently behind her hand, whereupon the gambler tapped the whiskey drummer on the shoulder. "Get rid of that." The drummer appeared startled. He grumbled, "Beg pardon," and tossed the smoke through the window.

All this while the coach went rushing down the ceaseless turns of the mountain road, rocking on its fore and aft springs, its heavy wheels slamming through the road ruts and whining on the curves. Occasionally the strident yell of Happy Stuart washed back. "Hi, Nelliel! By God –!" The whiskey drummer braced himself against the door and closed his eyes.

Three hours from Tonto the road, making a last round sweep, let them down upon the flat desert. Here the stage stopped and the men got out to stretch. The gambler spoke to the army girl, gently: "Perhaps you would find my seat, more comfortable." The army girl said, "Thank you," and changed over. The cavalry sergeant rode up to the stage, speaking to Happy Stuart.

"We'll be goin' back now – and good luck to ye."

The men piled in, the gambler taking the place beside Henriette. The blond man drew his long legs together to give the army girl more room, and watched Henriette's face with a soft, quiet care. A hard sun beat fully on the coach and dust began to whip up like fire smoke. Without escort they rolled across a flat earth broken only by cacti standing against a dazzling light. In the far distance, behind a blue heat haze, lay the faint suggestion of mountains.

The cattleman reached up and tugged at the ends of his mustache and smiled at Henriette. The army girl spoke to the blond man. "How far is it to the noon station?" The blond man said courteously: "Twenty miles." The gambler watched the army girl with the strictness of his face relaxing, as though the run of her voice reminded him of things long forgotten.

The miles fell behind and the smell of alkali dust got thicker. Henriette rested against the corner of the coach, her eyes dropped to the tips of her gloves. She made an enigmatic, disinterested shape there; she seemed past stirring, beyond laughter. She was young, yet she had a knowledge that put the cattleman and the gambler and the drummer and the army girl in their exact places; and she knew why the gambler had offered the army girl his seat. The army girl was in one world and she was in another, as everyone in the coach understood. It had no effect on her, for this was a distinction she had learned long ago. Only the blond man broke through her indifference. His name was Malpais Bill and she could see the wildness in the corners of his eyes and in the long crease of his lips; it was a stamp that would never come off. Yet something flowed out of him toward her that was different than the predatory curiosity of other men; something unobtrusively gallant, unexpectedly gentle.

Upon the box Happy Stuart pointed to the hazy outline two miles away. "Injuns ain't burned that anyhow." The sun was directly overhead, turning the light of the world a cruel brass-yellow. The crooked crack of a dry wash opened across the two deep ruts that made this road. Johnny Strang shifted the gun in his lap. "What's Malpais Bill ridin' with us for?"

"I guess I wouldn't ask him," returned Happy Stuart and

studied the wash with a troubled eye. The road fell into it roughly and he got a tighter grip on his reins and yelled: "Hang on! Hi, Nellie! God damn you, hi!" The six horses plunged down the rough side of the wash and for a moment the coach stood alone, high and lonely on the break, and then went reeling over the rim. It struck the gravel with a roar, the front wheels bouncing and the back wheels skewing around. The horses faltered but Happy Stuart cursed at his leaders and got them into a run again. The horses lunged up the far side of the wash two and two, their muscles bunching and the soft dirt flying in yellow clouds. The front wheels struck solidly and something cracked like a pistol shot; the stage rose out of the wash, teetered crosswise and then fell ponderously on its side, splintering the coach panels.

Johnny Strang jumped clear. Happy Stuart hung to the handrail with one hand and hauled on the reins with the other; and stood up while the passengers crawled through the upper door. All the men, except the whiskey drummer, put their shoulders to the coach and heaved it upright again. The whiskey drummer stood strangely in the bright sunlight shaking his head dumbly while the others climbed back in. Happy Stuart said, "All right, brother, git aboard."

The drummer climbed in slowly and the stage ran on. There was a low, grey dobe relay station squatted on the desert dead ahead with a scatter of corrals about it and a flag hanging limp on a crooked pole. Men came out of the dobe's dark interior and stood in the shade of the porch gallery. Happy Stuart rolled up and stopped. He said to a lanky man: "Hi, Mack. Where's the God-damned Injuns?"

The passengers were filing into the dobe's dining room. The lanky one drawled: "You'll see 'em before tomorrow night." Hostlers came up to change horses.

The little dining room was cool after the coach, cool and still. A fat Mexican woman ran in and out with the food platters. Happy Stuart said: "Ten minutes," and brushed the alkali dust from his mouth and fell to eating.

The long-jawed Mack said: "Catlin's ranch burned last night. Was a troop of cavalry around here yesterday. Came and went. You'll git to the Cap tonight all right but I do' know about the mountains beyond. A little trouble?"

"A little," said Happy briefly, and rose. This was the end of rest. The passengers followed, with the whisky drummer straggling at the rear, reaching deeply for wind. The coach rolled away again, Mack's voice pursuing them. "Hit it a lick, Happy, if you see any dust rollin' out of the east."

Heat had condensed in the coach and the little wind fanned up by the run of the horses was stifling to the lungs; the desert floor projected its white glitter endlessly away until lost in the smoky haze. The cattleman's knees bumped Henriette gently and he kept watching her, a celluloid toothpick drooped between his lips. Happy Stuart's voice ran back, profane and urgent, keeping the speed of the coach constant through the ruts. The whiskey drummer's eyes were round and strained and his mouth was open and all the colour had gone out of his face. The gambler observed this without expression and without care; and once the cattleman, feeling the sag of the whiskey drummer's shoulder, shoved him away. The Englishman sat bolt upright, staring emotionlessly at the passing desert. The army girl spoke to Malpais Bill: "What is the next stop?"

"Gap Creek."

"Will we meet soldiers there?"

He said: "I expect we'll have an escort over the hills into Lordsburg."

And at four o'clock of this furnace-hot afternoon the whiskey drummer made a feeble gesture with one hand and fell forward into the gambler's lap.

The cattleman shrugged his shoulders and put a head through the window, calling up to Happy Stuart. "Wait a minute." When the stage stopped everybody climbed out and the blond man helped the gambler lay the whiskey drummer in the sweltering patch of shade created by the coach. Neither Happy Stuart nor the shotgun guard bothered to get down. The whiskey drummer's lips moved a little but nobody said anything and nobody knew what to do – until Henriette stepped forward.

She dropped to the ground, lifting the whiskey drummer's shoulders and head against her breasts. He opened his eyes and there was something in them that they could all see, like relief and ease, like gratefulness. She murmured: "You are all right," and her smile was soft and pleasant, turning her lips maternal. There was this wisdom in her, this knowledge of the fears that men concealed behind their manners, the deep hungers that rode them so savagely, and the loneliness that drove them to women of her kind. She repeated, "You are all right," and watched this whiskey drummer's eyes lose the wildness of what he knew.

The army girl's face showed shock. The gambler and the cattleman looked down at the whiskey drummer quite impersonally. The blond man watched Henriette through lids half closed, but the flare of a powerful interest broke the severe lines of his cheeks. He held a cigarette between his fingers; he had forgotten it.

Happy Stuart said: "We can't stay here."

The gambler bent down to catch the whiskey drummer under the arms. Henriette rose and said, "Bring him to me," and got into the coach. The blond man and the gambler lifted the drummer through the door so that he was lying along the back seat, cushioned on Henriette's lap. They all got in and the coach rolled on. The drummer groaned a little, whispering: "Thanks – thanks," and the blond man, searching Henriette's face for every shred of expression, drew a gusty breath.

They went on like this, the big wheels pounding the ruts of the road while a lowering sun blazed through the coach windows. The mountain bulwarks began to march nearer, more definite in the blue fog. The cattleman's eyes were small and brilliant and touched Henriette personally, but the gambler bent toward Henriette to say: "If you are tired – " "No," she said. "No. He's dead."

The army girl stifled a small cry. The gambler bent nearer the whiskey drummer, and then they were all looking at Henriette; even the Englishman stared at her for a moment, faint curiosity in his eyes. She was remotely smiling, her lips broad and soft. She held the drummer's head with both her hands and continued to hold him like that until, at the swift fall of dusk, they rolled across the last of the desert floor and drew up before Gap Station.

The cattleman kicked open the door and stepped out, grunting as his stiff legs touched the ground. The gambler pulled the drummer up so that Henriette could leave. They all came out, their bones tired from the shaking. Happy Stuart climbed from the box, his face a grey mask of alkali and his eyes bloodshot. He said: "Who's dead?" and looked into the coach. People sauntered from the station yard, walking with the indolence of twilight. Happy Stuart said, "Well, he won't worry about tomorrow," and turned away.

A short man with a tremendous stomach shuffled through the dusk. He said: "Wasn't sure you'd try to git through yet, Happy."

"Where's the soldiers for tomorrow?"

"Other side of the mountains. Everybody's chased out. What ain't forted up here was sent into Lordsburg. You men will bunk in the barn. I'll make out for the ladies somehow." He looked at the army girl and he appraised Henriette instantly. His eyes slid on to Malpais Bill standing in the background and recognition stirred him then and made his voice careful. "Hello, Bill. What brings you this way?"

Malpais Bill's cigarette glowed in the gathering dusk and Henriette caught the brief image of his face, serene and watchful. Malpais Bill's tone was easy, it was soft. "Just the trip."

They were moving on toward the frame house whose corners seemed to extend indefinitely into a series of attached sheds. Lights glimmered in the windows and men moved around the place, idly talking. The unhitched horses went away at a trot. The tall girl walked into the station's big room, to face a soldier in a dishevelled uniform.

He said: "Miss Robertson? Lieutenant Hauser was to have met you here. He is at Lordsburg. He was wounded in a brush with the Apaches last night."

The tall army girl stood very still. She said: "Badly?"

"Well," said the soldier, "yes."

The fat man came in, drawing deeply for wind. "Too bad – too bad. Ladies, I'll show you the rooms, such as I got."

Henriette's dove-coloured dress blended with the background shadows. She was watching the tall army girl's face whiten. But there was a strength in the army girl, a fortitude that made her think of the soldier. For she said quietly, "You must have had a bad trip."

"Nothing – nothing at all," said the soldier and left the room. The gambler was here, his thin face turning to the army girl with a strained expression, as though he were remembering painful things. Malpais Bill had halted in the doorway, studying the softness and the humility of Henriette's cheeks. Afterwards both women followed the fat host of Gap Station along a narrow hall to their quarters.

Malpais Bill wheeled out and stood indolently against the wall of this desert station, his glance quick and watchful in the way it touched all the men loitering along the yard, his ears weighing all the night-softened voices. Heat died from the earth and a definite chill rolled down the mountain hulking sp high behind the house. The soldier was in his saddle, murmuring drowsily to Happy Stuart.

"Well, Lordsburg is a long ways off and the dam' mountains

are squirmin' with Apaches. You won't have any cavalry escort tomorrow. The troops are all in the field."

Malpais Bill listened to the hoofbeats of the soldier's horse fade out, remembering the loneliness of a man in those dark mountain passes, and went back to the saloon at the end of the station. This was a low-ceilinged shed with a dirt floor and whitewashed walls that once had been part of a stable. Three men stood under a lantern in the middle of this little place, the light of the lantern palely shining in the rounds of their eyes as they watched him. At the far end of the bar the cattleman and the gambler drank in taciturn silence. Malpais Bill took his whiskey when the bottle came, and noted the barkeep's obscure glance. Gap's host put in his head and wheezed, "Second table," and the other men in here began to move out. The barkeep's words rubbed together, one tone above a whisper. "Better not ride into Lordsburg. Plummer and Shanley are there."

Malpais Bill's lips were stretched to the long edge of laughter and there was a shine like wildness in his eyes. He said, "Thanks, friend," and went into the dining room.

When he came back to the yard night lay wild and deep across the desert and the moonlight was a frozen silver that touched but could not dissolve the world's incredible blackness. The girl Henriette walked along the Tonto road, swaying gently in the vague shadows. He went that way, the click of his heels on the hard earth bringing her around.

Her face was clear and strange and incurious in the night, as though she waited for something to come, and knew what it would be. But he said: "You're too far from the house. Apaches like to crawl down next to a settlement and wait for strays."

She was indifferent, unafraid. Her voice was cool and he could hear the faint loneliness in it, the fatalism that made her words so even. "There's a wind coming up, so soft and good."

He took off his hat, long legs braced, and his eyes were both attentive and puzzled. His blond hair glowed in the fugitive light.

She said in a deep breath: "Why do you do that?"

His lips were restless and the sing and rush of strong feeling was like a current of quick wind around him. "You have folks in Lordsburg?"

She spoke in a direct, patient way as though explaining something he should have known without asking. "I run a house in Lordsburg."

"No," he said, "it wasn't what I asked."

"My folks are dead – I think. There was a massacre in the Superstition Mountains when I was young."

He stood with his head bowed, his mind reaching back to fill in that gap of her life. There was a hardness and a rawness to this land and little sympathy for the weak. She had survived and had paid for her survival, and looked at him now in a silent way that offered no explanations or apologies for whatever had been; she was still a pretty girl with the dead patience of all the past years in her eyes, in the expressiveness of her lips.

He said: "Over in the Tonto Basin is a pretty land. I've got a piece of a ranch there – with a house half built."

"If that's your country, why are you here?"

His lips laughed and the rashness in him glowed hot again and he seemed to grow taller in the moonlight. "A debt to collect."

"That's why you're going to Lordsburg? You will never get through collecting those kind of debts. Everybody in the Territory knows you. Once you were just a rancher. Then you tried to wipe out a grudge and then there was a bigger one to wipe out - and the debt kept growing and more men are waiting to kill you. Someday a man will. You'd better run away from the debts."

His bright smile kept constant, and presently she lifted her shoulders with resignation. "No," she murmured, "you won't run." He could see the sweetness of her lips and the way her eyes were sad for him; he could see in them the patience he had never learned.

He said, "We'd better go back," and turned her with

his arm. They went across the yard in silence, hearing the undertone of men's drawling talk roll out of the shadows, seeing the glow of men's pipes in the dark corners. Malpais Bill stopped and watched her go through the station door; she turned to look at him once more, her eyes all dark and her lips softly sober, and then passed down the narrow corridor to her own quarters. Beyond her window, in the yard, a man was murmuring to another man: "Plummer and Shanley are in Lordsburg. Malpais Bill knows it." Through the thin partition of the adjoining room she heard the army girl crying with a suppressed, uncontrollable regularity. Henriette stared at the dark wall, her shoulders and head bowed; and afterwards returned to the hall and knocked on the army girl's door and went in.

Six fresh horses fiddled in front of the coach and the fat host of Gap Station came across the yard swinging a lantern against the dead, bitter black. All the passengers filed sleep-dulled and miserable from the house. Johnny Strang slammed the express box in the boot and Happy Stuart gruffly said: "All right, folks."

The passengers climbed in. The cattleman came up and Malpais Bill drawled: "Take the corner spot, mister," and got in, closing the door. The Gap host grumbled: "If they don't jump you on the long grade you'll be all right. You're safe when you get to Al Schrieber's ranch." Happy's bronze voice shocked the black stillness and the coach lurched forward, its leather springs squealing.

They rode for an hour in this complete darkness, chilled and uncomfortable and half asleep, feeling the coach drag on a heavy-climbing grade. Grey dawn cracked through, followed by a sunless light rushing all across the flat desert now far below. The road looped from one barren shoulder to another and at sunup they had reached the first bench and were slamming full speed along a boulder-strewn flat. The cattleman sat in the forward corner, the left corner of his mouth swollen and crushed, and when Henriette saw that her glance slid to Malpais Bill's knuckles. The army girl had her eyes closed, her shoulders pressing against the Englishman, who remained bolt upright with the sporting gun between his knees. Beside Henriette the gambler seemed to sleep, and on the middle bench Malpais Bill watched the land go by with a thin vigilance.

At ten they were rising again, with juniper and scrub pine showing on the slopes and the desert below them filling with the powdered haze of another hot day. By noon they reached the summit of the range and swung to follow its narrow rock-ribbed meadows. The gambler, long motionless, shifted his feet and caught the army girl's eyes.

"Schrieber's is directly ahead. We are past the worst of it."

The blond man looked around at the gambler, making no comment; and it was then that Henriette caught the smell of smoke in the windless air. Happy Stuart was cursing once more and the brake-blocks began to cry. Looking through he angled vista of the window panel Henriette saw a clay and rock chimney standing up like a gaunt skeleton against the day's light. The house that had been there was a black patch on the ground, smoke still rising from pieces that had not been completely burnt.

The stage stopped and all the men were instantly out. An iron stove squatted on the earth, with one section of pipe stuck upright to it. Fire licked lazily along the collapsed fragments of what had been a trunk. Beyond the location of the house, at the foot of a corral, lay two nude figures grotesquely bald, with deliberate knife slashes marking their bodies. Happy Stuart went over there and had his look; and came back.

"Schrieber's. Well –? "

Malpais Bill said: "This morning about daylight." He looked at the gambler, at the cattleman, at the Englishman who showed no emotion. "Get back in the coach." He climbed to the coach's top, flattening himself full length there. Happy Stuart and Strang took their places again. The horses broke into a run.

The gambler said to the army girl: "You're pretty safe

between those two fellows," and hauled a .44 from a back pocket and laid it over his lap. He considered Henriette more carefully than before, his taciturnity breaking. He said: "How old are you?"

Her shoulders rose and fell, which was the only answer. But the gambler said gently, "Young enough to be my daughter. It is a rotten world. When I call to you, lie down on the floor."

The Englishman had pulled the rifle from between his knees and laid it across the sill of the window on his side. The cattleman swept back the skirt of his coat to clear the holster of his gun.

The little flinty summit meadows grew narrower, with shoulders of grey rock closing in upon the road. The coach wheels slammed against the stony ruts and bounced high and fell again with ajar the springs could not soften. Happy Stuart's howl ran steadily above this rattle and rush. Fine dust turned all things grey.

Henriette sat with her eyes pinned to the gloved tips of her fingers, remembering the tall shape of Malpais Bill cut against the moonlight of Gap Station. He had smiled at her as a man might smile at any desirable woman, with the sweep and swing of laughter in his voice; and his eyes had been gentle. The gambler spoke very quietly and she didn't hear him until his fingers gripped her arm. He said again, not raising his voice: "Get down."

Henriette dropped to her knees, hearing gunfire blast through the rush and run of the coach. Happy Stuart ceased to yell and the army girl's eyes were round and dark. The walls of the canyon had tapered off. Looking upward through the window on the gambler's side, Henriette saw the weaving figure of an Apache warrior reel nakedly on a calico pony and rush by with a rifle raised and pointed in his bony elbows. The gambler took a cool aim; the stockman fired and aimed again. The Englishman's sporting rifle blasted heavy echoes through the coach, hurting her ears, and the smell of powder got rank and bitter. The blond man's boots scraped the coach top and round small holes began to dimple the panelling as the Apache bullets struck. An Indian came boldly abreast the coach and made a target that couldn't be missed. The cattleman dropped him with one shot. The wheels screamed as they slowed around the sharp ruts and the whole heavy superstructure of the coach bounced high into the air. Then they were rushing downgrade.

The gambler said quietly, "You had better take this," handing Henriette his gun. He leaned against the door with his small hands gripping the sill. Pallor loosened his cheeks. He said to the army girl: "Be sure and keep between those gentlemen," and looked at her with a way that was desperate and forlorn and dropped his head to the window's sill.

Henriette saw the bluff rise up and close in like a yellow wall. They were rolling down the mountain without brake. Gunfire fell off and the crying of the Indians faded back. Coming up from her knees then she saw the desert's flat surface far below, with the angular pattern of Lordsburg vaguely on the far borders of the heat fog. There was no more firing and Happy Stuart's voice lifted again and the brakes were screaming on the wheels, and going off, and screaming again. The Englishman stared out of the window sullenly; the army girl seemed in a deep desperate dream; the cattleman's face was shining with a strange sweat. Henriette reached over to pull the gambler up, but he had an unnatural weight to him and slid into the far corner. She saw that he was dead.

At five o'clock that long afternoon the stage threaded Lordsburg's narrow streets of dobe and frame houses, came upon the centre square and stopped before a crowd of people gathered in the smoky heat. The passengers crawled out stiffly. A Mexican boy ran up to see the dead gambler and began to yell his news in shrill Mexican. Malpais Bill climbed off the top, but Happy Stuart sat back on his seat and stared taciturnly at the crowd. Henriette noticed then that the shotgun messenger was gone.

A grey man in a sleazy white suit called up to Happy. "Well, you got through."

Happy Stuart said: "Yeah. We got through."

An officer stepped through the crowd, smiling at the army girl. He took her arm and said, "Miss Robertson, I believe. Lieutenant Hauser is quite all right. I will get your luggage – "

The army girl was crying then, definitely. They were all standing around, bone-weary and shaken. Malpais Bill remained by the wheel of the coach, his cheeks hard against the sunlight and his eyes riveted on a pair of men standing under the board awning of an adjoining store. Henriette observed the manner of their waiting and knew why they were here. The blond man's eyes, she noticed, were very blue and flame burned brilliantly in them. The army girl turned to Henriette, tears in her eyes. She murmured: "If there is anything I can ever do for you – "

But Henriette stepped back, shaking her head. This was Lordsburg and everybody knew her place except the army girl. Henriette said formally, "Goodbye," noting how still and expectant the two men under the awning remained. She swung toward the blond man and said, "Would you carry my valise?"

Malpais Bill looked at her, laughter remote in his eyes, and reached into the luggage pile and got her battered valise. He was still smiling as he went beside her, through the crowd and past the two waiting men. But when they turned into an anonymous and dusty little side street of the town, where the houses all sat shoulder to shoulder without grace or dignity, he had turned sober. He said: "I am obliged to you. But I'll have to go back there."

They were in front of a house no different from its neighbours; they had stopped at its door. She could see his eyes travel this street and comprehend its meaning and the kind of traffic it bore. But he was saying in that gentle, melody-making tone:

"I have watched you for two days." He stopped, searching his mind to find the thing he wanted to say. It came out swiftly. "God made you a woman. The Tonto is a pretty country."

Her answer was quite barren of feeling. "No. I am known all through the Territory. But I can remember that you asked me."

He said: "No other reason?" She didn't answer, but something in her eyes pulled his face together. He took off his hat and it seemed to her he was looking through this hot day to that far-off country and seeing it fresh and desirable. He murmured: "A man can escape nothing. I have got to do this. But I will be back."

He went along the narrow street, made a quick turn at the end of it and disappeared. Heat rolled like a heavy wave over Lordsburg's house tops and the smell of dust was very sharp.

She lifted her valise, and dropped it and stood like that, mute and grave before the door of her dismal house. She was remembering how tall he had been against the moonlight at Gap Station.

There were four swift shots beating furiously along the sultry quiet, and a shout, and afterwards a longer and longer silence. She put one hand against the door to steady herself, and knew that those shots marked the end of a man, and the end of a hope. He would never come back; he would never stand over her in the moonlight with the long gentle smile on his lips and with the swing of life in his casual tone. She was thinking of all that humbly and with the patience life had beaten into her . . .

She was thinking of all that when she heard the strike of boots on the street's packed earth; and turned to see him, high and square in the muddy sunlight, coming toward her with his smile.

DESTRY RIDES AGAIN

MAX BRAND

For seven days the wind came out of the north-east over the Powder Mountains and blew the skirts of a dust storm between Digger Hill and Bender Hill into the hollow where Lindsay was living in his shack. During that week Lindsay waked and slept with a piece of black coat-lining worn across his mouth and nostrils, but the dust penetrated like cosmic rays through the chinks in the walls of the cabin, through the mask and to the bottom of his lungs, so that every night he roused from sleep gasping for breath with a nightmare of being buried alive. Even lamplight could not drive that bad dream farther away than the misty corners of the room.

The blow began on a Tuesday morning, and by twilight of that day he knew what he was in for, so he went out through the whistling murk and led Jenny and Lind, his two mules, and Mustard, his old cream-coloured mustang, from the pasture into the barn. There he had in the mow a good heap of the volunteer hay which he had cut last May on the south-east forty, but the thin silt of the storm soon whitened the hay to such a degree that he had to shake it thoroughly before he fed the stock. Every two hours during that week, he roused himself by an alarm-clock instinct and went out to wash the nostrils and mouths of the stock, prying their teeth open and reaching right in to swab the black off their tongues. On Wednesday, Jenny, like the fool and villainess that she was, closed on his right forearm and raked off eight inches of skin.

Monotony of diet was more terrible to Lindsay than the storm. He had been on the point of riding to town and borrowing money from the bank on his growing crop so as to lay in a stock of provisions, but now he was confined with a bushel of potatoes and the heel of a side of bacon.

Only labour like that of the harvest field could make such food palatable and, in confinement as he was, never thoroughly stretching his muscles once a day, Lindsay began to revolt in belly and then in spirit. He even lacked coffee to give savour to the menu; he could not force himself more than once a day to eat potatoes, boiled or fried in bacon fat, with the dust gritting continually between his teeth.

He had no comfort whatever except for Caesar, his mongrel dog, and half a bottle of whiskey, from which he gave himself a nip once a day. Then in the night of the seventh day, there came to Lindsay a dream of a country where rolling waves of grass washed from horizon to horizon and all the winds of the earth could not blow a single breath of dust into the blue of the sky. He wakened with the dawn visible through the cracks in the shanty walls and a strange expectancy in his mind.

That singular expectation remained in him when he threw the door open and looked across the black of the hills toward the green light that was opening like a fan in the east; then he realised that it was the silence after the storm that seemed more enormous than all the stretch of landscape between him and the Powder Mountains. Caesar ran out past his legs to leap and bark and sneeze until something overawed him, in turn, and sent him skulking here and there with his nose to the ground as though he were following invisible bird trails. It was true that the face of the land was changed.

As the light grew Lindsay saw that the waterhole in the hollow was a black wallow of mud and against the woodshed leaned a sloping mass of dust like a drift of snow. The sight of this started him on the run for his eighty acres of winter-sown summer fallow. From a distance he saw the disaster but could not believe it until his feet were wading deep in the dust. Except for a few marginal strips, the whole swale of the ploughed land was covered with wind-filtered soil, a yard thick in the deepest places.

Two-thirds of his farm was wiped out, two-thirds of it was erased into permanent sterility; and the work of nearly ten years was entombed. He glanced down at the palms of his hands, for he was thinking of the burning, pulpy blisters that had covered them day after day when he was digging holes with the blunt post auger.

He looked up, then, at the distant ridges of the Powder Mountains. Ten years before in the morning light he had been able almost to count the great pines that walked up the slopes and stood on the mountains' crests, but the whole range had been cut over in the interim and the thick coat of forest which bound with its roots the accumulated soil of a million years had been mowed down. That was why the teeth of the wind had found substance they could eat into.

The entire burden of precious loam that dressed the mountains had been blown adrift in recent years and now the worthless underclay, made friable by a dry season, was laid in a stifling coat of silt across the farmlands of the lower valleys and the upper pastures of the range.

Lindsay did not think about anything for a time. His feet,

and an automatic impulse that made him turn always to the stock first, took him to the barn, where he turned loose the confined animals. Even the mules were glad enough to kick up their heels a few times, and fifteen years of hard living could not keep Mustard from exploding like a bomb all over the pasture, bucking as though a ghost were on his back and knocking up a puff of dust every time he hit the ground.

Lindsay, standing with feet spread and folded arms, a huge figure in the door of the barn, watched the antics of his old horse with a vacant smile, for he was trying to rouse himself and failing wretchedly. Instead, he could see himself standing in line with signed application slips in his hand, and then in front of a desk where some hired clerk with an insolent face put sharp questions to him. A month hence, when people asked him how things went, he would have to say, "I'm on the county."

When he had gone that far in his thinking, his soul at last rose in him but to such a cold, swift altitude that he was filled with fear, and he found his lips repeating words, stiffly, whispering them aloud, "I'll be damned and dead, first!" The fear of what he would do with his own hands grew stronger and stronger, for he felt that he had made a promise which would be heard and recorded by that living, inmost god of all honest men, his higher self.

Once more, automatically, his feet took him on to the

next step in the day: breakfast. Back in the shanty, his lips twitched with disgust as he started frying potatoes; the rank smell of the bacon grease mounted to his brain and gathered in clouds there, but his unthinking hands finished the cookery and dumped the fried potatoes into a tin plate.

A faint chorus came down to him then out of the windless sky. He snatched the loaded pistol from the holster that hung against the wall and ran outside, for sometimes the wild geese, flying north, came very low over the hill as they rose from the marsh south of it, but now he found himself agape like a schoolboy, staring up.

He should have known by the dimness of the honking and by the melancholy harmony which distance added to it that the geese were half a mile up in the sky. Thousands of them were streaming north in a great wedge that kept shuffling and reshuffling at the open ends; ten tons of meat on the wing.

A tin pan crashed inside the shack and Caesar came out on wings with his tail between his legs; Lindsay went inside and found the plate of potatoes overturned on the floor. He called, "Come in here, Caesar, you damned old thief. Come in here and get it, if you want the stuff. I'm better without."

The dog came back, skulking. From the doorway he prospected the face of his master for a moment, slavering with greed: then he sneaked to the food on the floor and began to eat guiltily, but Lindsay already had forgotten him. All through the hollow, which a week before had been a shining tremor of yellow green wheat stalks, the rising wind of the morning was now stirring little airy whirlpools and walking ghosts of dust that made a step or two and vanished.

It seemed to Lindsay that he had endured long enough. He was thirty-five. He had twenty years of hard work behind him. And he would not – by God, he would not - be a government pensioner! The wild geese had called the gun into his hand; he felt, suddenly, that it must be used for one last shot anyway. As for life, there was a stinking savour of bacon that clung inevitably to it. He looked with fearless eyes into the big muzzle of the gun.

Then Mustard whinnied not far from the house and Lindsay lifted his head with a faint smile, for there was a stallion's trumpet sound in the neigh of the old gelding, always, just as there was always an active devil in his heels and his teeth. He combined the savage instincts of a wildcat with the intellectual, patient malevolence of a mule, but Lindsay loved the brute because no winter cold was sharp enough to freeze the big heart in him and no dry summer march was long enough to wither it. At fifteen, the old fellow still could put fifty miles of hard country behind him between dawn and dark. For years Lindsay had felt that those long, mulish ears must eventually point the way to some great destiny.

He stepped into the doorway now and saw that Mustard was whinnying a challenge to a horseman who jogged up the Gavigan Trail with a telltale dust cloud boiling up behind. Mechanical instinct, again, made Lindsay drop the gun into the old leather holster that hung on the wall. Then he stepped outside to wait.

Half a mile off, the approaching rider put his horse into a lope and Lindsay recognised, by his slant in the saddle, that inveterate range tramp and worthless roustabout Gypsy Renner. He reined in at the door of the shack, lifted his bandana from nose and mouth and spat black.

"Got a drink, Bob?" he asked without other greeting.

"I've got a drink for you," said Lindsay.

"I'll get off a minute, then," replied Renner, and swung out of the saddle.

Lindsay poured some whiskey into a tin cup and Renner received it without thanks. Dust was still rising like thick smoke from his shoulders.

"You been far?" asked Lindsay.

"From Boulder," said Renner.

"Much of the range like out yonder?"

"Mostly," said Renner.

He finished the whiskey and held out the cup. Lindsay poured the rest of the bottle.

"If much of the range is like this," said Lindsay, "it's gonna be hell."

"It's gonna be and it is," said Renner. "It's hell already over on the Oliver Range."

"Wait a minute. That's where Andy Barnes and John Street run their cows. What you mean it's hell up there?"

"That's where I'm bound," said Renner. "They're hiring men and guns on both sides. Most of the waterholes and tanks on Andy Barnes's place are filled up with mud, right to the ridge of the Oliver Hills, and his cows are choking. And John Street, his land is clean because the wind kind of funnelled the dust up over the hills and it landed beyond him. Andy has to water those cows and Street wants to charge ten cents a head. Andy says he'll be damned if he pays money for the water that God put free on earth. So there's gonna be a fight."

Lindsay looked through the door at that lumpheaded mustang of his and saw, between his mind and the world, a moonlight night with five thousand head of cattle, market-fat and full of beans, stampeding into the northeast with a thunder and rattle of split hooves and a swordlike clashing of horns. He saw riders galloping ahead, vainly shooting into the face of the herd in the vain hope of turning it, until two of those cowpunchers, going it blind, clapped together and went down, head over heels.

"They used to be friends," said Lindsay. "They come so close to dying together, one night, that they been living side by side ever since; and they used to be friends."

"They got too damn rich," suggested Renner. "A rich man ain't nobody's friend . . . It was you that saved the two hides of them one night in a stampede, ten, twelve years ago, wasn't it?"

Lindsay pointed to Mustard.

"Now I'm gonna tell you something about that," he said. "The fact is that those cows would've washed right over the whole three of us, but I was riding that Mustard horse, and when I turned him back and pointed him at the herd, he just went off like a roman candle and scattered sparks right up to the Milky Way. He pitched so damn hard that he pretty near snapped my head off and he made himself look so big that those steers doggone near fainted and pushed aside from that spot."

Renner looked at the mustang with his natural sneer. Then he said, "Anyway, there's gonna be a fight up there, and it's gonna be paid for."

"There oughtn't be no fight," answered big Bob Lindsay, frowning.

"They're mean enough to fight," said Renner. "Didn't you save their scalps? And ain't they left you to starve here on a hundred and twenty acres of blowsand that can't raise enough to keep a dog fat?"

"Yeah?" said Lindsay. "Maybe you better be vamoosing along."

Renner looked at him, left the shack, and swung into the saddle. When he was safely there he muttered, "Ah, to hell with you!" and jogged away.

Lindsay, with a troubled mind, watched him out of sight. An hour later he saddled Mustard and took the way toward the Oliver Hills.

The Oliver Hills lie west of the Powder Mountains, their sides fat with grasslands all the way to the ridge, and right over the crest walked the posts of the fence that separated the holdings of Andy Barnes from those of John Street. Lindsay, as he came up the old Mexican Trail, stopped on a hilltop and took a careful view of the picture.

He had to strain his eyes a little because dust was blowing like battle smoke off the whitened acres of Andy Barnes and over the ridge, and that dust was stirred up by thousands of cattle which milled close to the fence line, drawn by the smell of water. Down the eastern hollows some of the beefs were wallowing in the holes where water once had been and where there was only mud now. But west of the ridge the lands of John Street were clean as green velvet under the noonday sun.

Scattered down the Street side of the fence, a score of

riders wandered up and down with significant lines of light balancing across the pommels of the saddles. Those were the rifles. As many more cowpunchers headed the milling cattle of Andy Barnes with difficulty, for in clear view of the cows, but on Street's side of the fence ran a knee-deep stream of silver water that spread out into a quiet blue lake, halfway down the slope.

He found a gate onto the Street land and went through it. Two or three of the line-riders hailed him with waving hats. One of them sang out, "Where's your rifle, brother? Men ain't worth a damn here without they got rifles."

He found John Street sitting on a spectacular black horse just west of a hilltop where the rise of land gave him shelter from ambitious sharpshooters. When he saw Lindsay, he grabbed him by the shoulders and bellowed like a bull in spring, "I knew you'd be over and I knew you'd be on the right side. By God, it's been eleven years since I was as glad to see you as I am today . . . Boys, I wanta tell you what Bob Lindsay here done for me when I got caught in – "

"Shut up, will you?" said Lindsay. "Looks like Andy has got some pretty dry cows, over yonder."

"I hope they dry up till there's nothing but wind in their bellies," said John Street.

"I thought you and Andy been pretty good friends," said Lindsay.

"If he was my brother – if he was two brothers – if he was my son and daughter and my pa and ma, he's so damn mean that I'd see him in hellfire before I'd give him a cup of water to wash the hellfire cinders out of his throat," said John Street, in part.

So Lindsay rode back to the gate and around to the party of Andy Barnes, passing steers with caked, dry mud of the choked waterholes layered around their muzzles. They were red-eyed with thirst and their bellowing seemed to rise like an unnatural thunder out of the ground instead of booming from the skies. Yearlings, already knock-kneed with weakness, were shouldered to the ground by the heavier stock and lay there, surrendering.

Andy Barnes sat cross-legged on the ground inside the rock circle of an old Indian camp on a hilltop, picking the grass, chewing it, spitting it out. He had grown much fatter and redder of face and the fat had got into his eyes, leaving them a little dull and staring.

Lindsay sat down beside him.

"You know something, Bob?" said Andy.

"Know what?" asked Lindsay.

"My wife's kid sister is over to the house," said Andy. "She's just turned twenty-three and she's got enough sense to cook a man steak and onions. As tall as your shoulder and the bluest dam' pair of eyes you ever seen outside a blind horse.

Never had bridle or saddle on her and I dunno how she'd go in harness, but you got a pair of hands. What you say? She's heard about Bob Lindsay for ten years, and she don't believe that there's that much man outside of a fairy story."

"Shut up, will you?" said Lindsay. "Seems like ten cents ain't much to pay for the difference between two thousand dead steers and two thousand dogies, all picking grass and fat and happy."

"Look up at that sky," said Andy.

"I'm looking," said Lindsay.

"Look blue?"

"Yeah. Kind of."

"Who put the blue in it?"

"God, maybe."

"Anybody ever pay him for it? And who put the water in the ground and made it leak out again? And why should I pay for *that*?"

"There's a lot of difference," said Lindsay, "between a dead steer on the range and a live steer in Chicago."

"Maybe," dreamed Andy, "but I guess they won't all be dead. You see that yearling over yonder, standing kind of spray-legged, with its nose pretty near on the ground?"

"I see it," said Lindsay.

"When that yearling kneels down," said Andy, "ther's gonna be something happen . . . Ain't that old Mustard?"

"Yeah, that's Mustard," said Lindsay, rising.

"If you ever get through with him," said Andy, "I got a lot of pasture land nothing ain't using where he could just range around and laugh himself to death. I ain't forgot when he was bucking the saddle off his back and knocking splinters out of the stars that night. He must've looked like a mountain to them steers, eh?"

Lindsay got on Mustard and rode over the hill. He went straight up to the fence which divided the two estates and dismounted before it with wire pincers in his hand. He felt scorn and uttermost detestation for the thing he was about to do. Men who cut fences are dirty rustlers and horse thieves and every man jack of them ought to be strung up as high as the top of the Powder Mountains; but the thirsty uproar of the cattle drove him onto what he felt was both a crime and a sin.

It had been a far easier thing, eleven years ago, to save Barnes and Street from the stampeding herd than it was to save them now from the petty hatred that had grown up between them without cause, without reason. The posts stood at such distance apart that the wires were strung with an extra heavy tension. When the steel edges cut through the topmost strand, it parted with a twang and leaped back to either side, coiling and tangling like thin, bright metallic snakes around the posts.

Yelling voices of protest came shouting through the dusty wind. Lindsay could see men dropping off their horses and lying prone to level their rifles at him; and all at once it seemed to him that the odour of frying bacon grease was thickening in his nostrils again and that this was the true savour of existence.

He saw the Powder Mountains lifting their sides from brown to blue in the distant sky with a promise of better lands beyond that horizon but the promise was a lie, he knew. No matter what he did, he felt assured that ten years hence he would be as now, a poor unrespected squatter on the range, slaving endlessly, not even for a monthly pay cheque, but merely to fill his larder with – bacon and Irish potatoes! Hope, as vital to the soul as breath to the nostrils, had been subtracted from him, and therefore what he did with his life was of no importance whatever. He leaned a little and snapped the pincers through the second wire of the fence.

He did not hear the sharp twanging sound of the parting strand, for a louder noise struck at his ear, a ringing rifle report full of resonance, like two heavy sledge-hammers struck face to face. At his feet a riffle of dust lifted; he heard the bullet hiss like a snake through the grass. Then a whole volley crashed. Bullets went by him on rising notes of enquiry; and just behind him a slug spatted into the flesh of

Mustard. Sometimes an axe makes a sound like that when it sinks into green wood.

He turned and saw Mustard sitting down like a dog, with his long, mulish ears pointing straight ahead and a look of pleased expectancy in his eyes. Out of a hole in his breast blood was pumping in long, thin jets.

Lindsay leaned and cut the third and last wire.

When he straightened again he heard the body of Mustard slump down against the ground with a squeaking, jouncing noise of liquids inside his belly. He did not lie on his side but with his head outstretched and his legs doubled under him as though he were playing a game and would spring up again in a moment.

Lindsay looked toward the guns. They never should have missed him the first time except that something like buck fever must have shaken the marksmen. He walked right through the open gap in the fence to meet the fire with a feeling that the wire clipper in his hand was marking him down like a cattle thief for the lowest sort of a death.

Then someone began to scream in a shrill falsetto. He recognised the voice of Big John Street, transformed by hysterical emotion. Street himself broke over the top of the hill with the black horse at a full gallop, yelling for his men to stop firing.

The wind of the gallop furled up the wide brim of his

sombrero and he made a noble picture, considering the rifles of Andy Barnes, which must be sighting curiously at him by this time; then a hammer stroke clipped Lindsay on the side of the head. The Powder Mountains whirled into a mist of brown and blue; the grass spun before him like running water; he dropped to his knees, and down his face ran a soft, warm stream.

Into his dizzy view came the legs and the sliding hooves of the black horse, cutting shallow furrows in the grass as it slid to a halt, and he heard the voice of John Street, dismounted beside him, yelling terrible oaths. He was grabbed beneath the armpits and lifted.

"Are you dead, Bob?" yelled Street.

"I'm gonna be all right," said Lindsay. He ran a fingertip through the bullet furrow in his scalp and felt the hard bone of the skull all the way. "I'm gonna be fine," he stated, and turned toward the uproar that was pouring through the gap he had cut in the fence.

For the outburst of rifle fire had taken the attention of Barnes's men from their herding and the cattle had surged past them toward water. Nothing now could stop that hungry stampede as they crowded through the gap with rattling hooves and the steady clashing of horns. Inside the fence the stream divided right and left and rushed on toward water, some to the noisy, white cataract, some to the wide blue pool.

"I'm sorry, John," said Lindsay, "but those cows looked kind of dry to me."

Then a nausea of body and a whirling dimness of mind overtook him and did not clear away again until he found himself lying with a bandaged head on the broad top of a hill. John Street was on one side of him and Andy Barnes on the other. They were holding hands like children and peering down at him anxiously.

"How are you, Bob, old son?" asked Andy.

"Fine," said Lindsay, sitting up. "Fine as a fiddle," he added, rising to his feet.

Street supported him hastily by one arm and Barnes by the other. Below him he could see the Barnes cattle thronging into the shallow water of the creek.

"About that ten cents a head," said Andy, "it's all right with me."

"Damn the money," said Street. "I wouldn't take money from you if you were made of gold . . . I guess Bob has paid for the water like he paid for our two hides eleven years ago. Bob, don't you give a hang about nothing? Don't you care nothing about your life?"

"The cows seemed kind of dry to me," said Lindsay, helplessly.

"You're comin' home with me," said Street.

"I got *two* females in my place to look after him," pointed out Andy Barnes.

"I got a cook that's a doggone sight better than a doctor," said Street.

"I don't need any doctor," said Lindsay. "You two just shut up and say goodbye to me, will you? I'm going home. I got work to do tomorrow."

This remark produced a silence out of which Lindsay heard, from the surrounding circle of cowmen, a voice that murmured, "He's gonna go home!" And another said, "He's got the chores to do, I guess."

Andy looked at John Street.

"He's gonna go, John," he said.

"There ain't any changing him," said John Street sadly. "Hey, Bob, take this here horse of mine, will you?"

"Doncha do it!" shouted Barnes. "Hey, Mickie, bring up that grey, will you? . . . Look at that piece of grey sky and wind, Bob, will you?"

"They're a mighty slick pair," said Lindsay. "I never seen a more upstanding pair of hellcats in my life. It would take a lot of barley and oats to keep them sleeked up so's they shine like this . . . But if you wanta wish a horse onto me, how about that down-headed, wise-lookin' cayuse over there? He's got some bottom to him and the hellfire is kind of worked out of his eyes."

He pointed to a brown gelding which seemed to have fallen half asleep. Another silence was spread by this remark. Then someone said: "He's picked out Slim's cuttin' horse . . . He's gone and picked out old Dick."

"Give them reins to Bob, Slim!" commanded Andy Barnes, "and leave the horse tied right onto the reins, too."

Lindsay said, "Am I parting you from something, Slim?"

Slim screwed up his face and looked at the sky.

"Why, I've heard about you, Lindsay," he said, "and today I've seen you. I guess when a horse goes to you, he's just going home; and this Dick horse of mine, I had the making of him and he sure rates a home . . . If you just ease him along the first half-hour, he'll be ready to die for you all the rest of the day."

"Thanks," said Lindsay, shaking hands. "I'm gonna value him, brother."

He swung into the saddle and waved his adieu. John Street followed him a few steps, and so did Andy Barnes.

"Are you gonna be comin' over? Are you gonna be comin' back, Bob?" they asked him.

"Are you two gonna stop being damn fools?" he replied.

They laughed and waved a cheerful agreement and they were still waving as he jogged Dick down the hill. The pain in his head burned him to the brain with every pulse of his blood but a strange feeling of triumph rose in his heart. He felt he never would be impatient again, for he could see that he was enriched for ever.

The twilight found him close to home and planning the work of the next days. If he put a drag behind the two mules he could sweep back the dust where it thinned out at the margin and so redeem from total loss a few more acres. With any luck, he would get seed for the next year; and as for food, he could do what he had scorned all his days – he could make a kitchen garden and irrigate it from the windmill.

It was dark when he came up the last slope and the stars rose like fireflies over the edge of the hill. Against them he made out Jenny and Lind waiting for him beside the door of the shack. He paused to stare at the vague silhouettes and remembered poor Mustard with a great stroke in his heart.

Caesar came with a shrill howl of delight to leap about his master and bark at the new horse, but Dick merely pricked his ears with patient understanding as though he knew he had come home indeed.

Inside the shanty the hand of Lindsay found the lantern. Lighting it brought a suffocating odor of kerosene fumes, but even through this Lindsay could detect the smell of fried bacon and potatoes in the air. He took a deep breath of it for it seemed to him the most delicious savour in the world.

WESTERN UNION

ZANE GREY

A voice on the wind whispered to Siena the prophecy of his birth. "A chief is born to save the vanishing tribe of Crows! A hunter to his starving people!" While he listened, at his feet swept swift waters, the rushing, green-white, thundering Athabasca, spirit-forsaken river; and it rumbled his name and murmured his fate. "Siena! Siena! His bride will rise from a wind kiss on the flowers in the moonlight! A new land calls to the last of the Crows! Northward where the wild goose ends its flight Siena will father a great people!"

So Siena, a hunter of the leafy trails, dreamed his dreams; and at sixteen he was the hope of the remnant of a once powerful tribe, a stripling chief, beautiful as a bronzed autumn god, silent, proud, forever listening to voices on the wind.

To Siena the lore of the woodland came as flight comes to the strong-winged wildfowl. The secrets of the forests were his, and of the rocks and rivers.

He knew how to find the nests of the plover, to call the loon, to net the heron and spear the fish. He understood the language of the whispering pines. Where the deer came down to drink and the caribou browsed on moss and the white rabbit nibbled in the grass and the bear dug in the logs for grubs – all these he learned; and also when the black flies drove the moose into the water and when the honk of the geese meant the approach of the north wind.

He lived in the woods, with his bow, his net and his spear. The trees were his brothers. The loon laughed for his happiness, the wolf mourned for his sadness. The bold crag above the river, Old Stoneface, heard his step when he climbed there in the twilight. He communed with the stern god of his ancestors and watched the flashing Northern Lights and listened.

From all four corners came his spirit guides with steps of destiny on his trail. On all the four winds breathed voices whispering of his future; loudest of all called the Athabasca, god-forsaken river, murmuring of the bride born of a wind kiss on the flowers in the moonlight.

It was autumn, with the flame of leaf fading, the haze rolling out of the hollows, the lull yielding to moan of coming wind. All the signs of a severe winter were in the hulls of the nuts, in the fur of the foxes, in the flight of waterfowl. Siena was spearing fish for winter store. None so keen of sight as Siena, so swift of arm; and as he was the hope, so he alone was the provider for the starving tribe. Siena stood to his knees in a brook where it flowed over its gravelly bed into the Athabasca. Poised high was his wooden spear. It glinted downward swift as a shaft of sunlight through the leaves. Then Siena lifted a quivering whitefish and tossed it upon the bank where his mother Ema, with other women of the tribe, sun-dried the fish upon a rock.

Again and again, many times, flashed the spear. The young chief seldom missed his aim. Early frosts on the uplands had driven the fish down to deeper water, and as they came darting over the bright pebbles Siena called them by name.

The oldest squaw could not remember such a run of fish. Ema sang the praises of her son; the other women ceased the hunger chant of the tribe.

Suddenly a hoarse shout pealed out over the waters.

Ema fell in a fright; her companions ran away; Siena leaped upon the bank, clutching his spear. A boat in which were men with white faces drifted down toward him.

"Hal-loa!" again sounded the hoarse cry.

Ema cowered in the grass. Siena saw a waving of white hands; his knees knocked together and he felt himself about to flee. But Siena of the Crows, the saviour of a vanishing tribe, must not fly from visible foes.

"Palefaces," he whispered, trembling, yet stood his ground ready to fight for his mother. He remembered stories of an old Indian who had journeyed far to the south and had crossed the trails of the dreaded white men. There stirred in him vague memories of strange Indian runners telling campfire tales of white hunters with weapons of lightning and thunder.

"Naza! Naza!" Siena cast one fleeting glance to the north and a prayer to his god of gods. He believed his spirit would soon be wandering in the shades of the other Indian world.

As the boat beached on the sand Siena saw men lying with pale faces upward to the sky, and voices in an unknown tongue greeted him. The tone was friendly, and he lowered his threatening spear. Then a man came up to the bank, his hungry eyes on the pile of fish, and he began to speak haltingly in mingled Cree and Chippewayan language:

"Boy - we're white friends – starving – let us buy fish - trade for fish - we're starving and we have many moons to travel."

"Siena's tribe is poor," replied the lad. "Sometimes they starve too. But Siena will divide his fish and wants no trade."

His mother, seeing the white men intended no evil, came out of her fright and complained bitterly to Siena of his liberality. She spoke of the menacing winter, of the frozen streams, the snow-bound forest, the long night of hunger. Siena silenced her and waved the frightened braves and squaws back to their wigwams.

"Siena is young," he said simply; "but he is chief here. If we starve – we starve."

Whereupon he portioned out a half of the fish. The white men built a fire and sat around it feasting like famished wolves around a fallen stag. When they had appeased their hunger they packed the remaining fish in the boat, whistling and singing the while. Then the leader made offer to pay, which Siena refused, though the covetous light in his mother's eyes hurt him sorely.

"Chief," said the leader, "the white man understands; now he offers presents as one chief to another."

Thereupon he proffered bright beads and tinselled trinkets, yards of calico and strips of cloth. Siena accepted with a dignity in marked contrast to the way in which the greedy Ema pounced upon the glittering heap. Next the paleface presented a knife which, drawn from its scabbard, showed a blade that mirrored its brightness in Siena's eyes.

"Chief, your woman complains of a starving tribe," went on the white man. "Are there not many moose and reindeer?"

"Yes. But seldom can Siena creep within range of his arrow."

"A-ha! Siena will starve no more," replied the man, and from the boat he took a long iron tube with a wooden stock.

"What is that?" asked Siena.

"The wonderful shooting stick. Here, boy, watch! See the bark on the campfire. Watch!"

He raised the stick to his shoulder. Then followed a streak of flame, a puff of smoke, a booming report; and the bark of the campfire flew into bits.

The children dodged into the wigwams with loud cries, the women ran screaming, Ema dropped in the grass wailing that the end of the world had come, while Siena, unable to move hand or foot, breathed another prayer to Naza of the northland.

The white man laughed and, patting Siena's arm, he said: "No fear." Then he drew Siena away from the bank, and began to explain the meaning and use of the wonderful shooting stick. He reloaded it and fired again and yet again, until Siena understood and was all aflame at the possibilities of such a weapon.

Patiently the white man taught the Indian how to load it, sight and shoot, and how to clean it with ramrod and buckskin. Next he placed at Siena's feet a keg of powder, a bag of lead bullets and boxes full of caps. Then he bade Siena farewell, entered the boat with his men and drifted round a bend of the swift Athabasca.

Siena stood alone upon the bank, the wonderful shooting stick in his hands, and the wail of his frightened mother in his ears. He comforted her, telling her the white men were gone, that he was safe, and that the prophecy of his birth had at last begun its fulfilment. He carried the precious ammunition to a safe hiding place in a hollow log near his wigwam and then he plunged into the forest.

Siena bent his course toward the runways of the moose. He walked in a kind of dream, for he both feared and believed. Soon the glimmer of water, splashes and widening ripples, caused him to crawl stealthily through the ferns and grasses to the border of a pond. The familiar hum of flies told him of the location of his quarry. The moose had taken to the water, driven by the swarms of black flies, and were standing neck deep, lifting their muzzles to feed on the drooping poplar branches. Their wide-spreading antlers, tipped back into the water, made the ripples.

Trembling as never before, Siena sank behind a log. He was within fifty paces of the moose. How often in that very spot had he strung a feathered arrow and shot it vainly! But now he had the white man's weapon, charged with lightning and thunder. Just then the poplars parted above the shore, disclosing a bull in the act of stepping down. He tossed his antlered head at the cloud of humming flies, then stopped, lifting his nose to scent the wind.

"Naza!" whispered Siena in his swelling throat.

He rested the shooting stick on the log and tried to see over the brown barrel. But his eyes were dim. Again he whispered a prayer to Naza. His sight cleared, his shaking arms stilled, and with his soul waiting, hoping, doubting, he aimed and pulled the trigger.

Boom!

High the moose flung his ponderous head, to crash down upon his knees, to roll in the water and churn a bloody foam, and then lie still.

"Siena! Siena!"

Shrill the young chiefs exultant yell pealed over the listening waters, piercing the still forest, to ring back in echo from Old Stoneface. It was Siena's triumphant call to his forefathers, watching him from the silence.

The herd of moose ploughed out of the pond and crashed into the woods, where, long after they had disappeared, their antlers could be heard cracking the saplings.

When Siena stood over the dead moose his doubts fled; he was indeed god-chosen. No longer chief of a starving tribe! Reverently and with immutable promise he raised the shooting stick to the north, toward Naza who had remembered him; and on the south, where dwelt the enemies of his tribe, his dark glance brooded wild and proud and savage.

Eight times the shooting stick boomed out in the stillness and eight moose lay dead in the wet grasses. In the twilight Siena wended his way home and placed eight moose tongues before the whimpering squaws.

"Siena is no longer a boy," he said. "Siena is a hunter. Let his women go bring in the meat."

Then to the rejoicing and feasting and dancing of his tribe he turned a deaf ear, and in the night passed alone under the shadow of Old Stoneface, where he walked with the spirits of his ancestors and believed the voices on the wind.

Before the ice locked the ponds Siena killed a hundred moose and reindeer. Meat and fat and oil and robes changed the world for the Crow tribe.

Fires burned brightly all the long winter; the braves awoke from their stupor and chanted no more; the women sang of the Siena who had come, and prayed for summer wind and moonlight to bring his bride.

Spring went by, summer grew into blazing autumn, and Siena's fame and wonder of the shooting stick spread through the length and breadth of the land.

Another year passed, then another, and Siena was the great chief of the rejuvenated Crows. He had grown into a warrior's stature, his face had the beauty of the god-chosen, his eye the falcon flash of the Sienas of old. Long communion in the shadow of Old Stoneface had added wisdom to his other gifts; and now to his worshipping tribe all that was needed to complete the prophecy of his birth was the coming of an alien bride.

It was another autumn, with the wind whipping the tamaracks and moaning in the pines, and Siena stole along a brown, fern-lined trail. The dry smell of fallen leaves filled his nostrils; he tasted snow in the keen breezes. The flowers were dead, and still no dark-eyed bride sat in his wigwam. Siena sorrowed and strengthened his heart to wait. He saw her flitting in the shadows around him, a wraith with dusky eyes veiled by dusky wind-blown hair, and ever she hovered near him, whispering from every dark pine, from every waving tuft of grass.

To her whispers he replied: "Siena waits."

He wondered of what alien tribe she would come. He hoped not of the unfriendly Chippewayans or the far-distant Blackfeet; surely not of the hostile Crees, life enemies of his tribe, destroyers of its once puissant strength, jealous now of its resurging power.

Other shadows flitted through the forest, spirits that rose silently from the graves over which he trod, and warned him of double steps on his trail, of unseen foes watching him from the dark coverts. His braves had repeated gossip, filterings from stray Indian wanderers, hinting of plots against the risen Siena. To all these he gave no heed, for was not he Siena, god-chosen, and had he not the wonderful shooting stick?

It was the season that he loved, when dim forest and hazy fernland spoke most impellingly. The tamaracks talked to him, the poplars bowed as he passed, and the pines sang for him alone. The dying vines twined about his feet and clung to him, and the brown ferns, curling sadly, waved him a welcome that was a farewell. A bird twittered a plaintive note and a loon whistled a lonely call. Across the wide grey hollows and meadows of white moss moaned the north wind, bending all before it, blowing full into Siena's face with its bitter promise. The lichen-covered rocks and the rugged-barked trees and the creatures that moved among them – the whole world of earth and air heard Siena's step on the rustling leaves and a thousand voices hummed in the autumn stillness.

So he passed through the shadowy forest and over the grey muskeg flats to his hunting place. With his birch-bark horn he blew the call of the moose. He alone of hunting Indians had the perfect moose call. There, hidden within a thicket, he waited, calling and listening till an angry reply bellowed from the depths of a hollow, and a bull moose, snorting fight, came cracking the saplings in his rush. When he sprang fierce and bristling into the glade, Siena killed him. Then, laying his shooting stick over a log, he drew his knife and approached the beast.

A snapping of twigs alarmed Siena and he whirled upon the defensive, but too late to save himself. A band of Indians pounced upon him and bore him to the ground. One wrestling heave Siena made, then he was overpowered and bound. Looking upward, he knew his captors, though he had never seen them before; they were the lifelong foes of his people, the fighting Crees.

A sturdy chief, bronze of face and sinister of eye, looked grimly down upon his captive. "Baroma makes Siena a slave."

Siena and his tribe were dragged far southward to the land of the Crees. The young chief was bound upon a block in the centre of the village where hundreds of Crees spat upon him, beat him and outraged him in every way their cunning could devise. Siena's gaze was on the north and his face showed no sign that he felt the torments.

At last Baroma's old advisers stopped the spectacle, saying: "This is a man!"

Siena and his people became slaves of the Crees. In Baroma's lodge, hung upon caribou antlers, was the wonderful shooting stick with Siena's powder horn and bullet pouch, objects of intense curiosity and fear.

None knew the mystery of this lightning-flashing,

thunder-dealing thing; none dared touch it.

The heart of Siena was broken; not for his shattered dreams or the end of his freedom, but for his people. His fame had been their undoing. Slaves to the murderers of his forefathers! His spirit darkened, his soul sickened; no more did sweet voices sing to him on the wind, and his mind dwelt apart from his body among shadows and dim shapes.

Because of his strength he was worked like a dog at hauling packs and carrying wood; because of his frame he was set to cleaning fish and washing vessels with the squaws. Seldom did he get to speak a word to his mother or any of his people. Always he was driven.

One day, when he lagged almost fainting, a maiden brought him water to drink. Siena looked up, and all about him suddenly brightened, as when sunlight bursts from cloud.

"Who is kind to Siena?" he asked, drinking.

"Baroma's daughter," replied the maiden.

"What is her name?"

Quickly the maiden bent her head, veiling dusky eyes with dusky hair. "Emihiyah."

"Siena has wandered on lonely trails and listened to voices not meant for other ears. He has heard the music of Emihiyah on the winds. Let the daughter of Siena's great foe not fear to tell of her name."

"Emihiyah means a wind kiss on the flowers in the moonlight," she whispered shyly and fled.

Love came to the last of the Sienas and it was like a glory. Death shuddered no more in Siena's soul. He saw into the future, and out of his gloom he rose again, god-chosen in his own sight, with such added beauty to his stern face and power to his piercing eye and strength to his lofty frame that the Crees quailed before him and marvelled. Once more sweet voices came to him, and ever on the soft winds were songs of the dewy moorlands to the northward, songs of the pines and the laugh of the loon and of the rushing, green-white, thundering Athabasca, god-forsaken river.

Siena's people saw him strong and patient, and they toiled on, unbroken, faithful. While he lived, the pride of Baroma was vaunting. "Siena waits" were the simple words he said to his mother, and she repeated them as wisdom. But the flame in his eye was like the leaping Northern Lights, and it kept alive the fire deep down in their breasts.

In the winter when the Crees lolled in their wigwams, when less labour fell to Siena, he set traps in the snow trails for silver fox and marten. No Cree had ever been such a trapper as Siena. In the long months he captured many furs, with which he wrought a robe the like of which had not before been the delight of a maiden's eye. He kept it by him for seven nights, and always during this time his ear was turned to the wind. The seventh night was the night of the midwinter feast, and when the torches burned bright in front of Baroma's lodge Siena took the robe and, passing slowly and stately till he stood before Emihiyah, he laid it at her feet.

Emihiyah's dusky face paled, her eyes that shone like stars drooped behind her flying hair, and all her slender body trembled.

"Slave!" cried Baroma, leaping erect. "Come closer that Baroma may see what kind of a dog approaches Emihiyah."

Siena met Baroma's gaze, but spoke no word. His gift spoke for him. The hated slave had dared to ask in marriage the hand of the proud Baroma's daughter. Siena towered in the firelight with something in his presence that for a moment awed beholders. Then the passionate and untried braves broke the silence with a clamour of the wolf pack.

Tillimanqua, wild son of Baroma, strung an arrow to his bow and shot into Siena's hip, where it stuck, with feathered shaft quivering.

The spring of the panther was not swifter than Siena; he tossed Tillimanqua into the air and, flinging him down, trod on his neck and wrenched the bow away. Siena pealed out the long-drawn war whoop of his tribe that had not been heard for a hundred years, and the terrible cry stiffened the Crees in their tracks.

Then he plucked the arrow from his hip and, fitting it to the string, pointed the gory flint head at Tillimanqua's eyes and began to bend the bow. He bent the tough wood till the ends almost met, a feat of exceeding great strength, and thus he stood with brawny arms knotted and stretched.

A scream rent the suspense. Emihiyah fell upon her knees. "Spare Emihiyah's brother!"

Siena cast one glance at the kneeling maiden, then, twanging the bowstring, he shot the arrow toward the sky.

"Baroma's slave is Siena," he said, with scorn like the lash of a whip. "Let the Cree learn wisdom."

Then Siena strode away, with a stream of dark blood down his thigh, and went to his brush tepee, where he closed his wound.

In the still watches of the night, when the stars blinked through the leaves and the dew fell, when Siena burned and throbbed in pain, a shadow passed between his weary eyes and the pale light. And a voice that was not one of the spirit voices on the wind called softly over him, "Siena! Emihiyah comes."

The maiden bound the hot thigh with a soothing balm and bathed his fevered brow.

Then her hands found his in tender touch, her dark face bent low to his, her hair lay upon his cheek. "Emihiyah keeps the robe," she said.

"Siena loves Emihiyah," he replied.

"Emihiyah loves Siena," she whispered.

She kissed him and stole away.

On the morrow Siena's wound was as if it had never been; no eye saw his pain. Siena returned to his work and his trapping. The winter melted into spring, spring flowered into summer, summer withered into autumn.

Once in the melancholy days Siena visited Baroma in his wigwam. "Baroma's hunters are slow. Siena sees a famine in the land."

"Let Baroma's slave keep his place among the squaws," was the reply.

That autumn the north wind came a moon before the Crees expected it; the reindeer took their annual march farther south; the moose herded warily in open groves; the whitefish did not run, and the seven-year pest depleted the rabbits.

When the first snow fell Baroma called a council and then sent his hunting braves far and wide.

One by one they straggled back to camp, footsore and hungry, and each with the same story. It was too late.

A few moose were in the forest, but they were wild and kept far out of range of the hunter's arrows, and there was no other game.

A blizzard clapped down upon the camp, and sleet and

snow whitened the forest and filled the trails. Then winter froze everything in icy clutch. The old year drew to a close.

The Crees were on the brink of famine. All day and all night they kept up their chanting and incantations and beating of tom-toms to conjure the return of the reindeer. But no reindeer appeared.

It was then that the stubborn Baroma yielded to his advisers and consented to let Siena save them from starvation by means of his wonderful shooting stick. Accordingly Baroma sent word to Siena to appear at his wigwam.

Siena did not go, and said to the medicine men: "Tell Baroma soon it will be for Siena to demand."

Then the Cree chieftain stormed and stamped in his wigwam and swore away the life of his slave. Yet again the wise medicine men prevailed. Siena and the wonderful shooting stick would be the salvation of the Crees. Baroma, muttering deep in his throat like distant thunder, gave sentence to starve Siena until he volunteered to go forth and hunt, or let him be the first to die.

The last scraps of meat, except a little hoarded in Baroma's lodge, were devoured, and then began the boiling of bones and skins to make a soup to sustain life. The cold days passed and a silent gloom pervaded the camp. Sometimes a cry of a bereaved mother, mourning for a starved child, wailed through the darkness. Siena's people, long used to starvation, did not suffer or grow weak so soon as the Crees. They were of hardier frame, and they were upheld by faith in their chief. When he would sicken it would be time for them to despair. But Siena walked erect as in the days of his freedom, nor did he stagger under the loads of firewood, and there was a light on his face. The Crees, knowing of Baroma's order that Siena should be the first to perish of starvation, gazed at the slave first in awe, then in fear. The last of the Sienas was succoured by the spirits.

But god-chosen though Siena deemed himself, he knew it was not by the spirits that he was fed in this time of famine. At night in the dead stillness, when even no mourning of wolf came over the frozen wilderness, Siena lay in his brush tepee close and warm under his blanket. The wind was faint and low, yet still it brought the old familiar voices. And it bore another sound – the soft fall of a moccasin on the snow. A shadow passed between Siena's eyes and the pale light.

"Emihiyah comes," whispered the shadow and knelt over him.

She tendered a slice of meat which she had stolen from Baroma's scanty hoard as he muttered and growled in uneasy slumber. Every night since her father's order to starve Siena, Emihiyah had made this perilous errand.

And now her hand sought his and her dusky hair swept his brow. "Emihiyah is faithful," she breathed low.

"Siena only waits," he replied.

She kissed him and stole away.

Cruel days fell upon the Crees, before Baroma's pride was broken. Many children died and some of the mothers were beyond help. Siena's people kept their strength, and he himself showed no effect of hunger. Long ago the Cree women had deemed him superhuman, that the Great Spirit fed him from the happy hunting grounds.

At last Baroma went to Siena. "Siena may save his people and the Crees."

Siena regarded him long, then replied: "Siena waits."

"Let Baroma know. What does Siena wait for? While he waits we die."

Siena smiled his slow, inscrutable smile and turned away.

Baroma sent for his daughter and ordered her to plead for her life.

Emihiyah came, fragile as a swaying reed, more beautiful than a rose choked in a tangled thicket, and she stood before Siena with doe eyes veiled. "Emihiyah begs Siena to save her and the tribe of Crees."

"Siena waits," replied the slave.

Baroma roared his fury and bade his braves lash the slave. But the blows fell from feeble arms and Siena laughed at his captors.

Then, like a wild lion unleashed from long thrall, he

turned upon them: "Starve! Cree dogs! Starve! When the Crees all fall like leaves in autumn, then Siena and his people will go back to the north."

Baroma's arrogance left him then, and on another day, when Emihiyah lay weak and palid in his wigwam and the pangs of hunger gnawed at his own vitals, he again sought Siena. "Let Siena tell for what he waits."

Siena rose to his lofty height and the leaping flame of the Northern Light gathered in his eyes. "Freedom!" One word he spoke and it rolled away on the wind.

"Baroma yields," replied the Cree, and hung his head. "Send the squaws who can walk and the braves who can crawl out upon Siena's trail."

Then Siena went to Baroma's lodge and took up the wonderful shooting stick and, loading it, he set out upon snowshoes into the white forest. He knew where to find the moose yards in the sheltered corners. He heard the bulls pounding the hard-packed snow and cracking their antlers on the trees. The wary beasts would not have allowed him to steal close, as a warrior armed with a bow must have done, but Siena fired into the herd at long range. And when they dashed off, sending the snow up like a spray, a huge black bull lay dead. Siena followed them as they floundered through the drifts, and whenever he came within range he shot again. When five moose were killed he turned upon his trail to find almost the whole Cree tribe had followed him and were tearing the meat and crying out in a kind of crazy joy. That night the fires burned before the wigwams, the earthen pots steamed and there was great rejoicing. Siena hunted the next day, and the next, and for ten days he went into the white forest with his wonderful shooting stick, and eighty moose fell to his unerring aim.

The famine was broken and the Crees were saved.

When the mad dances ended and the feasts were over, Siena appeared before Baroma's lodge. "Siena will lead his people northward."

Baroma, starving, was a different chief from Baroma well fed and in no pain. All his cunning had returned. "Siena goes free. Baroma gave his word. But Siena's people remain slaves."

"Siena demanded freedom for himself and his people," said the younger chief.

"Baroma heard no word of Siena's tribe. He would not have granted freedom for them. Siena's freedom was enough."

"The Cree twists the truth. He knows Siena would not go without his people. Siena might have remembered Baroma's cunning. The Crees were ever liars."

Baroma stalked before his fire with haughty presence. About him in the circle of light sat his medicine men, his braves and squaws. "The Cree is kind. He gave his word.

Siena is free. Let him take his wonderful shooting stick and go back to the north."

Siena laid the shooting stick at Baroma's feet and likewise the powder horn and bullet pouch. Then he folded his arms, and his falcon eyes looked far beyond Baroma to the land of the changing lights and the old home on the green-white, rushing Athabasca, god-forsaken river. "Siena stays."

Baroma started in amazement and anger. "Siena makes Baroma's word idle. Begone!"

"Siena stays!"

The look of Siena, the pealing reply, for a moment held the chief mute. Slowly Baroma stretched wide his arms and lifted them, while from his face flashed a sullen wonder. "Great Slave!" he thundered.

So was respect forced from the soul of the Cree, and the name thus wrung from his jealous heart was one to live for ever in the lives and legends of Siena's people.

Baroma sought the silence of his lodge, and his medicine men and braves dispersed, leaving Siena standing in the circle, a magnificent statue facing the steely north.

From that day insult was never offered to Siena, nor word spoken to him by the Crees, nor work given. He was free to come and go where he willed, and he spent his time in lessening the tasks of his people.

The trails of the forest were always open to him, as were the streets of the Cree village. If a brave met him, it was to step aside; if a squaw met him, it was to bow her head; if a chief met him, it was to face him as warriors faced warriors.

One twilight Emihiyah crossed his path, and suddenly she stood as once before, like a frail reed about to break in the wind. But Siena passed on. The days went by and each one brought less labour to Siena's people, until that one came wherein there was no task save what they set themselves. Siena's tribe were slaves, yet not slaves.

The winter wore by and the spring and the autumn, and again Siena's fame went abroad on the four winds. The Chippewayans journeyed from afar to see the Great Slave, and likewise the Blackfeet and the Yellow Knives. Honour would have been added to fame; councils called; overtures made to the sombre Baroma on behalf of the Great Slave, but Siena passed to and fro among his people, silent and cold to all others, true to the place which his great foe had given him. Captive to a lesser chief, they said; the Great Slave who would yet free his tribe and gather to him a new and powerful nation.

Once in the late autumn Siena sat brooding in the twilight by Ema's tepee. That night all who came near him were silent. Again Siena was listening to voices on the wind, voices that had been still for long, which he had tried to forget. It was the north wind, and it whipped the spruces and moaned through the pines. In its cold breath it bore a message to Siena, a hint of coming winter and a call from Naza, far north of the green-white, thundering Athabasca, river without a spirit.

In the darkness when the camp slumbered Siena faced the steely north. As he looked a golden shaft, arrow-shaped and arrow-swift, shot to the zenith.

"Naza!" he whispered to the winds. "Siena watches."

Then the gleaming, changing Northern Lights painted a picture of gold and silver bars, of flushes pink as shell, of opal fire and sunset red; and it was a picture of Siena's life from the moment the rushing Athabasca rumbled his name, to the far distant time when he would say farewell to his great nation and pass for ever to the retreat of the winds. God-chosen he was, and had power to read the story in the sky.

Seven nights Siena watched in the darkness; and on the seventh night, when the golden flare and silver shafts faded in the north, he passed from tepee to tepee, awakening his people. "When Siena's people hear the sound of the shooting stick let them cry greatly: Siena kills Baroma! Siena kills Baroma!"

With noiseless stride Siena went among the wigwams and along the lanes until he reached Baroma's lodge. Entering the dark he groped with his hands upward to a moose's antlers and found the shooting stick. Outside he fired it into the air.

Like a lightning bolt the report ripped asunder the silence, and the echoes clapped and reclapped from the cliffs. Sharp on the dying echoes Siena bellowed his war whoop, and it was the second time in a hundred years for foes to hear that terrible, long-drawn cry.

Then followed the shrill yells of Siena's people: "Siena kills Baroma . . . Siena kills Baroma . . . Siena kills Baroma!"

The slumber of the Crees awoke to a babel of many voices; it rose hoarsely on the night air, swelled hideously into a deafening roar that shook the earth.

In this din of confusion and terror when the Crees were lamenting the supposed death of Baroma and screaming in each other's ears, "The Great Slave takes his freedom!" Siena ran to his people and, pointing to the north, drove them before him.

Single file, like a long line of flitting spectres, they passed out of the fields into the forest. Siena kept close on their trail, ever looking backward, and ready with the shooting stick.

The roar of the stricken Crees softened in his ears and at last died away.

Under the black canopy of whispering leaves, over the

grey, mist-shrouded muskeg flats, around the glimmering reed-bordered ponds, Siena drove his people.

All night Siena hurried them northward and with every stride his heart beat higher. Only he was troubled by a sound like a voice that came to him on the wind.

But the wind was now blowing in his face, and the sound appeared to be at his back. It followed on his trail as had the step of destiny. When he strained his ears he could not hear it, yet when he had gone on swiftly, persuaded it was only fancy, then the voice that was not a voice came haunting him.

In the grey dawn Siena halted on the far side of a grey flat and peered through the mists on his back trail. Something moved out among the shadows, a grey shape that crept slowly, uttering a mournful cry.

"Siena is trailed by a wolf," muttered the chief.

Yet he waited, and saw that the wolf was an Indian. He raised the fatal shooting stick.

As the Indian staggered forward, Siena recognised the robe of silver fox and marten, his gift to Emihiyah. He laughed in mockery. It was a Cree trick. Tillimanqua had led the pursuit disguised in his sister's robe. Baroma would find his son dead on the Great Slave's trail.

"Siena!" came the strange, low cry.

It was the cry that had haunted him like the voice on the

wind. He leaped as a bounding deer.

Out of the grey fog burned dusky eyes half veiled by dusky hair, and little hands that he knew wavered as fluttering leaves. "Emihiyah comes," she said.

"Siena waits," he replied.

Far to the northward he led his bride and his people, far beyond the old home on the green-white, thundering Athabasca, god-forsaken river; and there, on the lonely shores of an inland sea, he fathered the Great Slave Tribe.

THE VIRGINIAN

Owen Wister

Scipio Le Moyne lay in bed, held together with bandages. His body had need for many bandages. A Bar-Circle-Zee three-year-old had done him violent mischief at the forks of Stinking Water. But for the fence, Scipio might have swung clear of the wild, rearing animal. When they lifted his wrecked frame from the ground, one of them had said: "A spade's all he'll need now."

Overhearing this with some still unconquered piece of his mind, Scipio made one last remark: "I ain't going to die for years and years."

Upon this his head had rolled over, and no further statements came from him for – I forget how long. Yet somehow, we all believed that last remark of his.

"Since I've known him," said the Virginian, "I have found him a truthful man."

"Which don't mean," Honey Wiggin put in, "that he can't lie when he ought to."

Judge Henry always sent his hurt cowpunchers to the nearest surgical aid, which in this case was the hospital on the reservation. Here then, one afternoon, Scipio lay, his body still bound tight at a number of places, but his brain needing no bandages whatever; he was able to see one friend for a little while each day. It was almost time for this day's visitor to go, and the visitor looked at his watch.

"Oh, don't do that!" pleaded the man in bed. "I'm not sick any more."

"You will be sick some more if you keep talking," replied the Virginian.

"Thinkin' is a heap more dangerous, if y'u can't let it out," Scipio urged. "I'm not half through tellin' y'u about Horacles."

"Did his mother name him that?" enquired the Virginian.

"Naw! but his mother brought it on him. Didn't y'u know? Of course you don't often get so far north in the Basin as the Agency. His name is Horace Pericles Byram. Well, the Agent wasn't going to call his assistant store-clerk all that, y'u know, not even if he *has* got an uncle in the Senate of the United States. Couldn't spare the time. Days not long enough. Not even in June. So everybody calls him Horacles now. He's reconciled to it. But I ain't. It's too good for him. A heap too good. I've knowed him all my life, and I can't think of a name that's not less foolish than he is. Well, where was I? I was tellin' y'u how back in Gallipo*leece* he couldn't understand anything. Not dogs. Not horses. Not girls."

"Do you understand girls?" the Virginian interrupted.

"Better'n Horacles. Well, now it seems he can't understand Indians. Here he is sellin' goods to 'em across the counter at the Agency store. I could sell twiced what he does, from what they tell me. I guess the Agent has begun to discover what a trick the Uncle played him when he unloaded Horacles on him. Now why did the Uncle do that?"

Scipio stopped in his rambling discourse, and his brows knitted as he began to think about the Uncle. The Virginian once again looked at his watch, but Scipio, deep in his thoughts, did not notice him. "Uncle," he resumed to himself, half aloud, "Uncle was the damnedest scoundrel in Gallipo*leece*. – Say!" he exclaimed suddenly, and made an eager movement to sit up. "Oh Lord!" he groaned, sinking back. "I forgot – what's your hurry?"

But the Virginian had seen the pain transfix his friend's face, and though that face had instantly smiled, it was white. He stood up. "I'd ought to get kicked from here to the ranch," he said, remorsefully. "I'll get the doctor."

Vainly the man in bed protested; his visitor was already

at the door.

"I've not told y'u about his false teeth!" shrieked Scipio, hoping this would detain him. "And he does tricks with a rabbit and a bowl of fish."

But the guest was gone. In his place presently the Post surgeon came, and was not pleased. Indeed, this excellent army doctor swore. Still, it was not the first time that he had done so, nor did it prove the last; and Scipio, it soon appeared, had given himself no hurt. But in answer to a severe threat, he whined: "Oh, ain't y'u goin' to let me see him tomorro'?"

"You'll see nobody tomorrow except me."

"Well, that'll be seein' nobody," whined Scipio, more grievously.

The doctor grinned. "In some ways you're incurable. Better go to sleep now." And he left him.

Scipio did not go to sleep then, though by morning he had slept ten healthful hours, waking with the Uncle still at the centre of his thoughts. It made him again knit his brows.

"No, you can't see him today," said the doctor, in reply to a request.

"But I hadn't finished sayin' something to him," Scipio protested. "And I'm well enough to see my dead grandmother."

"That I'll not forbid," answered the doctor. And he added that the Virginian had gone back to Sunk Creek with some horses.

"Oh, yes," said Scipio. "I'd forgot. Well, he'll be coming through on his way to Billings next week. You been up to the Agency lately? Yesterday? Well, there's going to be something new happen. Agent seem worried or anything?"

"Not that I noticed. Are the Indians going on the warpath?"

"Nothing like that. But why does a senator of the United States put his nephew in that store? Y'u needn't to tell me it's to provide for him, for it don't provide. I thought I had it figured out last night, but Horacles don't fit. I can't make him fit. He don't understand Injuns. That's my trouble. Now the Uncle must know Horacles don't understand. But if he didn't know?" pursued Scipio, and fell to thinking.

"Well," said the doctor indulgently, as he rose, "it's good you can invent these romances. Keeps you from fretting, shut up here alone."

"There'd be no romances here," retorted Scipio. "Uncle is exclusively hard cash." The doctor departed.

At his visit next morning, he was pleased with his patient's condition. "Keep on," said he, "and I'll let you sit up Monday for ten minutes. Any more romances?"

"Been thinkin' of my past life," said Scipio.

The doctor laughed long. "Why, how old are you, anyhow?" he asked at length.

"Oh, there's some lovely years still to come before I'm thirty. But I've got a whole lot of past life, all the same." Then he pointed a solemn, oracular finger at the doctor. "What white man sawys the Injun? Not you. Not me. And I've drifted around some, too. The map of the United States has been my home. Been in Arizona and New Mexico and among the Siwashes – seen all kinds of Injun – but I don't sawy 'em. I know most any Injun's better'n most any white man till he meets the white man. Not smarter, y'u know, but better. And I do know this: you take an Injun and let him be a warrior and a chief and a grandfather who has killed heaps of white men in his day – but all that don't make him grown up. Not like we're grown up. He stays a child in some respects till he's dead. He'll believe things and be scared at things that ain't nothin' to you and me. You take Old High Bear right on this reservation. He's got hair like snow and eyes like an eagle's and he can sing a war-song about fights that happened when our fathers were kids. But if you want to deal with him, you got to remember he's a child of five."

"I do know all this," said the doctor, interested. "I've not been twenty years on the frontier for nothing."

"Horacles don't know it," said Scipio. "I've saw him in the store all season."

"Well," said the doctor, "see you tomorrow. I've some new patients in the ward."

"Soldiers?"

"Soldiers."

"Guess I know why they're here."

"Oh, yes," sighed the doctor. "You know. Few come here for any other reason." The doctor held views about how a military post should be regulated, which popular sentiment will never share. "Can I do anything for you?" he inquired.

"If I could have some newspapers?" said Scipio.

"Why didn't you tell me before?" said the doctor. After that he saw to it that Scipio had them liberally.

With newspapers the patient sat surrounded deep, when the Virginian, passing north on his way to Billings, looked in for a moment to give his friend the good word. That is what he came for, but what he said was: "So he has got false teeth?"

Scipio, hearing the voice at the door, looked over the top of his paper at the visitor.

"Yes," he replied, precisely as if the visitor had never been out of the room.

"What d' y'u know?" inquired the Virginian.

"Nothing; what do you?"

"Nothing."

After all, such brief greetings cover the ground.

117

"Better sit down," suggested Scipio.

The Virginian sat, and took up a paper. Thus for a little while they both read in silence.

"Did y'u stop at the Agency as y'u came along?" asked Scipio, not looking up from his paper.

"No."

There was silence again as they continued reading. The Virginian, just come from Sunk Creek, had seen no newspapers as recent as these. When two friends on meeting after absence can sit together for half an hour without a word passing between than, it is proof that they really enjoy each other's company. The gentle air came in the window, bringing the tonic odour of the sage-brush. Outside the window stretched a yellow world to distant golden hills. The talkative voice of a magpie somewhere near at hand was the only sound.

"Nothing in the newspapers in particular," said Scipio, finally.

"You expaictin' something particular?" the Virginian asked.

"Yes."

"Mind sayin' what it is?"

"Wish I knew what it is."

"Always Horacles?"

"Always him – and Uncle. I'd like to spot Uncle."

Mess call sounded from the parade ground. It recalled the flight of time to the Virginian.

"When you get back from Billings," said Scipio, "you're liable to find me up and around."

"Hope so. Maybe you'll be well enough to go with me to the ranch."

But when the Virginian returned, a great deal had happened all at once, as is the custom of events.

Scipio's vigorous convalescence brought him in the next few days to sitting about in the open air, and then enlarged his freedom to a crutch. He hobbled hither and yon, paying visits, many of them to the doctor. The doctor it was, and no newspaper, who gave to Scipio the first grain of that 'something particular' which he had been daily seeking and never found. He mentioned a new building that was being put up rather far away down in the corner of the reservation. The rumor in the air was that it had something to do with the Quartermaster's department. The odd thing was that the Quartermaster himself had heard nothing about it. The Agent up at the Agency store considered this extremely odd. But a profound absence of further explanations seemed to prevail. What possible need for a building was there at that inconvenient, isolated spot?

Scipio slapped his leg. "I guess what y'u call my romance is about to start."

"Well," the doctor admitted, "it may be. Curious things are done upon Indian reservations. Our management of them may be likened to putting the Lord's Prayer and the Ten Commandments into a bag and crushing them to powder. Let our statesmen at Washington get their hands on an Indian reservation, and not even honour among thieves remains."

"Say, doc," said Scipio, "when d' y'u guess I can get off?"

"Don't be in too much of a hurry," the doctor cautioned him. "If you go to Sunk Creek –"

"Sunk Creek! I only want to go to the Agency."

"Oh, well, you could do that today – but don't you want to see the entertainment? Conjuring tricks are promised."

"I want to see Horacles."

"But he is the entertainment. Supper comes after he's through."

Scipio stayed. He was not repaid, he thought. "A poor show," was his comment as he went to bed. He came later to be very glad indeed that he had gone to that entertainment.

The next day found him seated in the Agency store, being warmly greeted by his friends the Indians. They knew him well; perhaps he understood them better than he had said. By Horacles he was not warmly greeted; perhaps Horacles did not wish to be understood – and then, Scipio, in his comings and goings through the reservation, had played with

Horacles for the benefit of bystanders. There is no doubt whatever that Horacles did not understand Scipio. He was sorry to notice how the Agent, his employer, shook Scipio's hand and invited him to come and stop with him till he was fit to return to his work. And Scipio accepted this invitation. He sat him down in the store, and made himself at home. Legs stretched out on one chair, crutch within reach, hands comfortably clasped round the arms of the chair he sat in, head tilted back, eyes apparently studying the goods which hung from the beams overhead, he visibly sniffed the air.

"Smell anything you don't like?" enquired the clerk, tartly – and unwisely.

"Nothin' except you, Horacles," was the perfectly amiable rejoinder. "It's good," Scipio then confessed, "to be smellin' buckskin and leather and groceries instead of ether and iodoform."

"Guess you were pretty sick," observed the clerk, with relish.

"Yes. Oh, yes. I was pretty sick. That's right. Yes." Scipio had continued through these slowly drawled remarks to look at the ceiling. Then his glance dropped to the level of Horacles, and keenly fixed that unconscious youth's plump little form, pink little face and mean little mustache. Behind one ear stuck a pen, behind the other a pencil, as the assistant clerk was arranging some tins of Arbuckle's Arioso coffee.

Then Scipio took aim and fired: "So you're going to quit your job?"

Horacles whirled round. "Who says so?"

The chance shot – if there ever is such a thing, if such shots are not always the result of visions and perceptions which lie beyond our present knowledge – this chance shot had hit.

"First I've heard of it," then said Horacles, sulkily. "Guess you're delirious still." He returned to his coffee, and life grew more interesting than ever to Scipio.

Instead of trickling back, health began to rush back into his long imprisoned body, and though he could not fully use it yet, and though if he hobbled a hundred yards he was compelled to rest it, his wiry mind knew no fatigue. How athletic his brains were was easily perceived by the Indian Agent. The convalescent would hobble over to the store after breakfast and hail the assistant clerk at once. "Morning, Horacles," he would begin; "how's Uncle?" – "Oh, when are you going to give us a new joke?" the worried Horacles would retort. – "Just as soon as you give us a new Uncle, Horacles. Or any other relation to make us feel proud we know you. What did his letter last night say?" The second or third time this had been asked still found Horacles with no better repartee than angry silence. "Didn't he send me his love?" Scipio then said; and still the hapless Horacles said nothing. "Well, y'u give him mine when you write him this afternoon." – "I ain't writing this afternoon," snapped the clerk. – "You're not! Why, I thought you wrote each other every day!" This was so near the truth that Horacles flared out: "I'd be ashamed if I'd nothing better to do than spy on other people's mails."

Thus by dinner time generally an audience would be gathered round Scipio where he sat with his legs on the chair, and Horacles over his ledger would be furiously muttering that "Some day they would all see."

Horacles asked for a couple of days' holiday, and got it. He wished to hunt, he said. But the Agent happened to find that he had been to the railroad about some freight. This he mentioned to Scipio. "I don't know what he's up to," he said. He had found that worrying Horacles was merely one of the things that Scipio's brains were good for; Scipio had advised him prudently about a sale of beeves, and had introduced a simple contrivance for luring to the store the customers whom Horacles failed to attract. It was merely a free lunch counter – cheese and crackers every day, and deviled ham on pay-day – but it put up the daily receipts.

And next, one evening after the mail was in, Scipio, sitting alone in the front of the store, saw the Agent, sitting alone in the back of the store, spring suddenly from his chair, crush a newspaper into his pocket, and stride out to his house.

At breakfast the Agent spoke thus to Scipio: "I must go to Washington. I shall be back before they let you and your leg run loose. Will you do something for me?"

"Name it. Just name it."

"Run the store while I'm gone."

"D' y'u think I can?"

"I know you can. There'll be no trouble under you. You understand Indians."

"But suppose something turns up?"

"I don't think anything will before I'm back. I'd sooner leave you than Horacles in charge here. Will you do it and take two dollars a day?"

"Do it for nothing. Horacles'll be compensation enough."

"No, he won't – and see here, he can't help being himself."

"Enough said. I'll strive to pity him. None of us was consulted about being born. And I'll keep remembering that we was both raised at Gallipol*eece*, Ohio, and that he inherited a bigger outrage of a name than I did. That's what comes of havin' a French ancestor – only, he used to steal my lunch at school." And Scipio's bleached blue eye grew cold. Later injuries one may forgive, but school ones never.

"Didn't you whale him?" asked the Agent.

"Every time," said Scipio, "till he told Uncle. Uncle was

mayor of Gallipol*eece* then. So I wasn't ready to get expelled – I got ready later; nothin' is easier than gettin' expelled – but I locked up my lunch after that."

"Uncle's pretty good to him," muttered the Agent. "Got him this position – well, nobody will expel you here. Look after things. I'll feel easy to think you're on hand."

For that newspaper which the Agent had crushed into his pocket, Scipio searched cracks and corners, but searched in vain. A fear quite unreasoning possessed him for a while: could he but learn what was in the paper that had so stirred his patron, perhaps he could avert whatever the thing was that he felt in the air, threatening some sort of injury. He knew himself resourceful. Dislike of Horacles and Uncle had been enough to start his wish to thwart them – if there was anything to thwart; but now pride and gratitude fired him; he had been trusted; he cared more to be trusted than for anything on earth; he must rise equal to it now! The Agent had evidently taken the paper away with him – and so Scipio absurdly read all the papers. He collected old ones, and laid his hands upon the new the moment they were out of the mailbag. It may be said that he lived daily in a wrapping of newspapers.

"Why, you have got Horacles laughing at you."

This the observant Virginian pointed out to Scipio immediately on his arrival from Billings. Scipio turned a sickened look upon his friend. The look was accompanied by a cold wave in his stomach.

"Y'u cert'nly have," the remorseless friend pursued. "I reckon he must have had a plumb happy time watchin' y'u still-hunt them newspapers. Now who'd ever have foretold you would afford Horacles enjoyment?"

In a weak voice Scipio essayed to fight it off. "Don't you try to hoodwink me with any of your frog lies."

"No need," said the Virginian. "From the door as I came in I saw him at his desk lookin' at y'u easy-like. 'Twas a right quaint pictyeh – him smilin' at the desk, and your nose tight agaynst the Omaha *Bee*. I thought first y'u didn't have a handkerchief."

"I wonder if he has me beat?" muttered poor Scipio.

The Virginian now had a word of consolation. "Don't y'u see," he again pointed out, "that no newspaper could have helped you? If it could why did he go away to Washington without tellin' you? He don't look for you to deal with troubles he don't mention to you."

"I wonder if Horacles has me beat?" said Scipio once more.

The Virginian standing by the seated, brooding man clapped him twice on the shoulders, gently. It was enough. They were very fast friends.

"I know," said Scipio in response. "Thank y'u. But I'd hate

for him to have me beat."

It was the doctor who now furnished information that would have relieved any reasonable man from a sense of failure. The doctor was excited because his view of our faith in Indian matters was again justified by a further instance.

"Oh, yes! he said. "Just give those people at Washington time, and every step they've taken from the start will be in the mud puddle of a lie. Uncle's in the game all right. He's been meditating how to serve his country and increase his income. There's a railroad at the big end of his notion, but the entering wedge seems only to be a new store down in the corner of this reservation. You see, it has been long settled by the sacredest compacts that two stores shall be enough here – the Post-trader's and the Agent's – but the dear Indians need a third, Uncle says. He has told the Senate and the Interior Department and the White House that a lot of them have to travel too far for supplies. So now Washington is sure the Indians need a third store. The Post-trader and the Agent are stopping at the Post tonight. They got East too late to hold up the job. If Horacles opens that new store, the Agent might just as well shut up his own."

"Ain't y'u going to look at my leg?" was all the reply that Scipio made.

The doctor laughed. It was to examine the leg that he had come, and he had forgotten all about it. "You can forget all about it, too," he told Scipio when he had finished. "Go back to Sunk Creek when you like. Go back to full work next week, say. Your wicked body is sound again. A better man would unquestionably have died."

But the cheery doctor could not cheer the unreasonable Scipio. In the morning the complacent little Horacles made known to all the world his perfected arrangements. Directly the Agent had safely turned his back and gone to Washington, his disloyal clerk had become doubly busy. He had at once perceived that this was a comfortable time for him to hurry his new rival store into readiness and be securely established behind its counter before his betrayed employer should return. In this last he might not quite succeed; the Agent had come back a day or two sooner than Horacles had calculated, but it was a trifle; after all, he had carried through the small part of his uncle's scheme which he had been sent here to do. Inside that building in the far corner of the reservation, once rumoured to be connected with the Quartermaster's department, he would now sell luxuries and necessities to the Indians at a price cheaper than his employer's, and his employer's store would henceforth be empty of customers. Perhaps the sweetest moment that Horacles had known for many weeks was when he said to Scipio: "I'm writing Uncle about it today."

That this should have gone on under his nose while he sat

searching the papers was to Scipio utterly unbearable. His mind was in a turmoil, feeling about helplessly but furiously for vengeance; and the Virginian's sane question – What could he have done to stop it if he had discovered it? – comforted him not at all. They were outside the store, sitting under a tree, waiting for the returning Agent to appear. But he did not come, and the suspense added to Scipio's wretchedness.

"He put me in charge," he kept repeating.

"The driver ain't responsible when a stage is held up," reasoned the Virginian.

Scipio hardly heard him. "He put me in charge," he said. Then he worked round to Horacles again. "He ain't got strength. He ain't got beauty. He ain't got riches. He ain't got brains. He's just got sense enough for parlour conjuring tricks – not good ones, either. And yet he has me beat."

"He's got an uncle in the Senate," said the Virginian.

The disconsolate Scipio took a pull at his cigar – he had taken one between every sentence. "Damn his false teeth."

The Virginian looked grave. "Don't be hasty. Maybe the day will come when you and me'll need 'em to chew our tenderloin."

"We'll be old. Horacles is twenty-five."

"Twenty-five is certainly young to commence eatin' by machinery," admitted the Virginian.

"And he's proud of 'em," whined Scipio. "Proud! Opens

his bone box and sticks 'em out at y'u on the end of his tongue."

"I hate an immodest man," said the Virginian.

"Why, he hadn't any better sense than to do it over to the officers' club right before the ladies and everybody the other night. The KO's wife said it gave her the creeps – and she don't look sensitive."

"Well," said the Virginian, "if I weighed three hundred pounds I'd be turrable sensitive."

"She had to leave," pursued Scipio. "Had to take her little girl away from the show. Them teeth comin' out of Horacles's mouth the way they did sent the child into hysterics. Y'u could hear her screechin' halfway down the line."

The Virginian looked at his watch. "I wonder if that Agent is coming here at all today?"

Scipio's worried face darkened again. "What can I do? What *can* I?" he demanded. And he rose and limped up and down where the ponies were tied in front of the store. The fickle Indians would soon be tying these ponies in front of the rival store. "I received this business in good shape," continued Scipio, "and I'll hand it back in bad."

Horacles looked out of the door. He wore his hat tilted to make him look like the daredevil that he was not; daredevils seldom have soft pink hands, red eyelids and a fluffy mustache. He smiled at Scipio, and Scipio smiled at him, sweetly and dangerously.

"Would you mind keeping store while I'm off?" enquired Horacles.

"Sure not!" cried Scipio, with heartiness. "Goin' to have your grand opening this afternoon?"

"Well, I *was*," Horacles replied, enjoying himself every moment. "But Mr Forsythe" (this was the Agent) "can't get over from the Post in time to be present this afternoon. It's very kind of him to want to be present when I start my new enterprise, and I appreciate it, boys, I can tell you. So I sent him word I wouldn't think of opening without him, and it's to be tomorrow morning."

While Horacles was speaking thus, the Indians had gathered about to listen. It was plain that they understood that this was a white man's war; their great, grave, watching faces showed it. Young squaws, half-hooded in their shawls, looked on with bright eyes; a boy who had been sitting out on the steps playing a pipe, stopped his music, and came in; the aged Pounded Meat, wrapped in scarlet and shrunk with years to the appearance of a dried apple, watched with eyes that still had in them the primal fire of life; tall in a corner stood the silver-haired High Bear, watching too. Did they understand the white man's war lying behind the complacent smile of Horacles and the dangerous smile of the lounging Scipio? The red man is grave when war is in question; all the

Indians were perfectly still.

"Wish you boys could be there to give me a good send-off," continued Horacles.

The pipe-playing Indian boy must have caught some flash of something beneath Scipio's smile, for his eye went to Scipio's pistol – but it returned to Scipio's face.

Horacles spoke on. "Fine line of fresh Eastern goods, dry goods, candies, and – hee-hee! – free lunch. Mr Le Moyne, I want to thank you publicly for that idea."

"Y'u're welcome to it. Guess I'll hardly be over tomorrow, though. With such a competitor as you, I expect I'll have to stay with my job and hustle."

"Ah, well," simpered Horacles, "I couldn't have done it by myself. My Uncle – say, boys!" (Horacles in the elation of victory now melted to pure goodwill) "Do come see me tomorrow. It's all business, this, you know. There's no hard feelings?"

The pipe boy couldn't help looking at the pistol again.

"Not a feeling!" cried Scipio. And he clapped Horacles between his little round shoulders. With head on one side, he looked down along his lengthy, jocular nose at Horacles for a moment. Then his eye shone upon the company like the edge of a knife – and they laughed at him because he was laughing so contagiously at them; a soft laugh, like the fall of moccasins. Often the Indian will join, like a child, in mirth which he does not comprehend. High Bear's smile shone from his corner at young Scipio, whom he fancied so much that he had offered him his fourteenth daughter to wed as soon as his leg should be well. But Scipio had sorrowfully explained to the father that he was already married – which was true, but which I fear would in former days have proved no impediment to him. Perhaps some day I may tell you of the early marriages of Scipio as Scipio in hospital narrated them to me.

"Hey!" said High Bear now, to Scipio. "New store. Pretty good. Heap cheap."

"Yes, High Bear. Heap cheap. You savvy why?"

With a long arm and an outstretched finger, Scipio suddenly pointed to Horacles. At this the Virginian's hitherto unchanging face wakened to curiosity and attention. Scipio was now impressively and mysteriously nodding at the silver-haired chief in his bright, green blanket, and his long, fringed, yellow, soft buckskins.

"No savvy," said High Bear, after a pause, with a tinge of caution. He had followed Scipio's pointing finger to where Horacles was happily practising a trick with a glass and a silver dollar behind the counter.

"Heap cheap," repeated Scipio, "because" (here he leaned close to High Bear and whispered) "because his uncle medicine-man. He big medicine-man, too."

High Bear's eyes rested for a moment on Horacles. Then he shook his head. "Ah, nah," he grunted. "He not medicine-man. He fall off horse. He no catch horse. My little girl catch him. Ah, nah!" High Bear laughed profusely at 'Sippo's' joke. 'Sippo' was the Indians' English name for their vivacious friend. In their own language they called him something complimentary in several syllables, but it was altogether too intimate and too plain-spoken for me to repeat aloud. Into his whisper Scipio now put more electricity. "He's big medicine-man," he hissed again, and he drilled his bleached blue eye into the brown one of the savage. "See him now!" He stretched out a vibrating finger.

It was a pack of cards that Horacles was lightly manipulating. He fluttered it open in the air and fluttered it shut again, drawing it out like a concertina and pushing it flat like an opera hat – nor did a card fall to the ground.

High Bear watched it hard; but soon High Bear laughed. "He pretty good," he declared. "All same tin-horn monte-man. I see one Miles City."

"Maybe monte-man medicine-man too," suggested Scipio.

"Ah, nah!" said High Bear. Yet nevertheless Scipio saw him shoot one or two more doubtful glances at Horacles as that happy clerk continued his activities.

Horacles had an audience (which he liked), and he held

his audience – and who could help liking that? The bucks
and squaws watched him, sometimes nudging one another,
and they smiled and grunted their satisfaction at his news.
Cheaper prices was something which their primitive minds
could take in as well as any of us.

"Why you not sell cheap like him?" they asked their
friend 'Sippo'. "We stay then. Not go his store." This was
the burden of their chorus, soft, laughing, a little mocking,
floating among them like a breeze, voice after voice:

"We like buy everything you, we like buy everything
cheap."

"You make cheap, we buy heap shirts."

"Buy heap tobacco."

"Heap cartridge."

"You not sell cheap, we go."

"Ah!"

The chorus laughed like pleased children.

Scipio looked at them solemnly. He explained how much
he would like to sell cheap, if only he were a medicine-man
like Horacles.

"You medicine-man?" they asked the assistant clerk.

"Yes," said Horacles, pleased. "I big medicine-man."

"Ah, nah!" The soft, mocking words ran among them like
the flight of a moth.

Soon with their hoods over their heads they began to go

home on their ponies, blanketed, feathered, many-coloured, moving and dispersing wide across the sage-brush to their far-scattered tepees.

High Bear lingered last. For a long while he had been standing silent and motionless. When the chorus spoke he had not; when the chorus laughed he had not. Now his head moved; he looked about him and saw that for a moment he was alone in a way. He saw the Virginian reading a newspaper, and his friend 'Sippo' bending down and attending to his leg. Horacles had gone into an inner room. Left on the counter lay the pack of cards. High Bear went quickly to the cards, touched them, lifted them, set them down and looked about him again. But the Virginian was reading still, and Scipio was still bent down, having some trouble with his boot. High Bear looked at the cards, shook his head sceptically, laughed a little, grunted once, and went out where his pony was tied. As he was throwing his soft buckskin leg over the saddle, there was Scipio's head thrust out of the door and nodding strangely at him.

"Goodnight, High Bear. He big medicine-man."

High Bear gave a quick slash to his pony, and galloped away into the dusk.

Then Scipio limped bade into the store, sank into the first chair he came to, and doubled over. The Virginian looked up from his paper at this mirth, scowled, and turned back to his reading. If he was to be 'left out' of the joke, he would make it plain that he was not in the least interested in it.

Scipio now sat up straight, bursting to share what was in his mind; but he instantly perceived how it was with the Virginian. At this he redoubled his silent symptoms of delight. In a moment Horacles had come back from the inner room with his hair wet with ornamental brushing.

"Well, Horacles," began Scipio in the voice of a purring cat, "I expect y'u have me beat."

The flattered clerk could only nod and show his bright, false teeth.

"Y'u have me beat," repeated Scipio. "Y'u have for a fact."

"Not you, Mr Le Moyne. It's not you I'm making war on. I do hope there's no hard feelings –"

"Not a feelin', Horacles! How can y'u entertain such an idea?" Scipio shook him by the hand and smiled like an angel at him – a fallen angel. "What's the use of me keepin' this store open tomorrow? Nobody'll be here to spend a cent. Guess I'll shut up, Horacles, and come watch the Injuns all shoppin' like Christmas over to your place."

The Virginian sustained his indifference, and added to Scipio's pleasure. But during breakfast the Virginian broke down.

"Reckon you're ready to start today?" he said.

"Start? Where for?"

"Sunk Creek, y'u fool! Where else?"

"I'm beyond y'u! I'm sure beyond y'u for once!" screeched Scipio, beating his crutch on the floor.

"Oh, eat your grub, y'u fool."

"I'd have told y'u last night," said Scipio, remorselessly, "only y'u were so awful anxious not to *be* told."

As the Virginian drove him across the sage-brush, not to Sunk Creek, but to the new store, the suspense was once more too much for the Southerner's curiosity. He pulled up the horses as the inspiration struck him.

"You're going to tell the Indians you'll undersell him!" he declared, over-hastily.

"Oh, drive on, y'u fool," said Scipio.

The baffled Virginian grinned. "I'll throw you out," he said, "and break all your laigs and bones and things fresh."

"I wish Uncle was going to be there," said Scipio.

Nearly everybody else was there: the Agent, bearing his ill fortune like a philosopher, some officers from the Post, and the doctor; some enlisted men, blue-legged with yellow stripes; civilians male and female, honourable and shady; and then the Indians. Wagons were drawn up, ponies stood about, the littered plain was populous. Horacles moved behind the counter, busy and happy; his little mustache was combed, his ornamental hair was damp. He smiled and talked, and handled and displayed his abundance: the bright calicoes, the shining knives, the clean six-shooters and rifles, the bridles, the fishing-tackle, the gum-drops and chocolates – all his plenty and its cheapness.

Squaws and bucks young and old thronged his establishment, their soft footfalls and voices made a gentle continuous sound, while their green and yellow blankets bent and stood straight as they inspected and purchased. High Bear held an earthen crock with a luxury in it – a dozen of fresh eggs. "Hey!" he said when he saw his friend 'Sippo' enter. "Heap cheap." And he showed the eggs to Scipio. He cherished the crock with one hand and arm while with the other hand he helped himself to the free lunch.

To Scipio Horacles 'extended' a special welcome; he made it otentatious in order that all the world might know how perfectly absent 'hard feelings' were. And Scipio on his side wore openly the radiance of brotherhood and well-wishing. He went about admiring everything, exclaiming now and then over the excellence of the goods, or the cheapness of their price. His presence was soon no longer a cause of curiosity, and they forgot to watch him – all of them except the Virginian. The hours passed on, the little fires, where various noon meals were cooked, burnt out, satisfied individuals began to depart after an entertaining day, the Agent himself was sauntering toward his horse.

"What's your hurry?" said Scipio.

"Well, the show is over," said the Agent.

"Oh, no, it ain't. Horacles is goin' to entertain us a whole lot."

"Better stay," said the Virginian.

The Agent looked from one to the other. Then he spoke anxiously. "I don't want anything done to Horacles."

"Nothing will be done," stated Scipio.

The Agent stayed. The magnetic current of expectancy passed, none could say how, through the assembled people. No one departed after this, and the mere loitering of spectators turned to waiting. Particularly expectant was the Virginian, and this he betrayed by mechanically droning in his strongest accent a little song that bore no reference to the present occasion:

"Of all my fatheh's familee
I love myself the baist,
And if Gawd will just look afteh me
The devil may take the raist."

The sun grew lower. The world outside was still full of light, but dimness had begun its subtle pervasion of the store. Horacles thanked the Indians and every one for their generous patronage on this his opening day, and intimated that it was time to close. Scipio rushed up and whispered to him: "My goodness, Horacles! You ain't going to send your friends home like that?"

Horacles was taken aback. "Why," he stammered, "what's wrong?"

"Where's your vanishing handkerchief, Horacles? Get it out and entertain 'em some. Show you're grateful. Where's that trick dollar? Get 'em quick – I tell you," he declaimed aloud to the Indians, "he big medicine-man. Make come. Make go. You no see. Nobody see. Make jack-rabbit in hat –"

"I couldn't tonight," simpered Horacles. "Needs preparation, you know." And he winked at Scipio.

Scipio struggled upon the counter, and stood up above their heads to finish his speech. "No jack-rabbit this time," he said.

"Ah, nah!" laughed the Indians. "No catch um."

"Yes, catch um any time. Catch anything. Make anything. Make all this store" – Scipio moved his arms about – "that's how make heap cheap. See that!" He stopped dramatically, and clasped his hands together. Horacles tossed a handkerchief in the air, caught it, shut his hand upon it with a kneading motion, and opened the hand empty. "His fingers swallow it, all same mouth!" shouted Scipio. "He big medicine-man. You see. Now other hand spit out." But Horacles varied the trick. Success and the staring crowd elated him; he was going to do his best. He opened both hands empty, felt about him in the air, clutched space suddenly, and drew two silver dollars from it. Then he threw them back into space, again felt about for them in the air, made a dive at High Bear's eggs, and brought handkerchief and dollars out of them.

"Ho!" went High Bear, catching his breath. He backed away from the reach of Horacles. He peered down into the crock among his eggs. Horacles whispered to Scipio: "Keep talking till I'm ready."

"Oh, I'll talk. Go get ready quick – High Bear, what I tell you?" But High Bear's eye was now fixedly watching the door through which Horacles had withdrawn; he did not listen as Scipio proceeded. "What I tell everybody? He do handkerchief. He do dollar. He do heap more. See me. I no can do tike him. I not medicine-man. I throw handkerchief and dollar in the air, look! See! they tumble on floor no good – thank you, my kind noble friend from Virginia, you pick my fool dollar and my fool handkerchief up for me, *muy pronto*. Oh, thank you, blackhaired, green-eyed son of Dixie, you have the manners of a queen, but I no medicine-man, I shall never turn a skunk into a watermelon, I innocent, I young, I helpless babe, I suck bottle when I can get it. Fire and water will not obey me. Old man Makes-the-Thunder does not know my name and address. He spit on me Wednesday night last, and there are no dollars in this man's hair." (The Virginian winced beneath Scipio's vicious snatch at his scalp, and the Agent and the doctor retired to a dark corner and laid their heads in each other's waistcoats.) "Ha! he comes! Big medicine-man comes. See him, High Bear! His father, his mother, his aunts all twins, he ninth dog-pup in three sets of triplets, and the great white Ram-of-the-Mountains fed him on punkin-seed – sick 'em, Horacles."

The burning eye of High Bear now blazed with distended fascination, riveted upon Horacles, whom it never left. Darkness was gathering in the store.

"Hand all same foot," shouted Scipio, with gestures, "mouth all same hand. Can eat fire. Can throw ear mile off and listen you talk." Here Horacles removed a dollar from the hair of High Bear's fourteenth daughter, threw it into one boot, and brought it out of the other. The daughter screamed and burrowed behind her sire. All the Indians had drawn close together, away from the counter, while Scipio on top of the counter talked high and low, and made gestures without ceasing. "Hand all same mouth. Foot all same head. Take off head, throw it out window, it jump in door. See him, see big medicine-man!" And Scipio gave a great shriek.

A gasp went among the Indians; red fire was blowing from the jaws of Horacles. It ceased, and after it came slowly, horribly, a long red tongue, and riding on the tongue's end glittered a row of teeth. There was a crash upon the floor. It was High Bear's crock. The old chief was gone. Out of the door he flew, his blanket over his face, and up on his horse he sprang, wildly beating the animal. Squaws and bucks flapped after him like poultry, rushing over the ground, leaping on their ponies, melting away into the dusk. In a moment no sign of them was left but the broken eggs, oozing about on the deserted floor.

The white men there stood tearful, dazed and weak with laughter.

" 'Happy-Teeth' should be his name," said the Virginian. "It sounds Injun." And Happy-Teeth it was. But Horacles did not remain long in the neighbourhood after he realised what he had done; for never again did an Indian enter, or even come near, that den of flames and magic. They would not even ride past it; they circled it widely. The idle merchandise that filled it was at last bought by the Agent at a reduction.

"Well," said Scipio bashfully to the Agent, "I'd have sure hated to hand y'u back a ruined business. But he'll never understand Injuns."

CLARENCE E. MULFORD

Clarence E. Mulford was born in 1883. He started writing at a young age, creating Hopalong Cassidy, the fictional cowboy that would make his name, in the 1907 novel *Bar 20*. Hopalang went on to star in numerous short stories and 28 novels, culminating with *Hopalong Cassidy Serves a Writ* (1941). The cowboy was made even more famous, however, by the 66 Hopalong Cassidy films he starred in, which were produced over a 13-year period with almost no input from Mulford.

O. HENRY

William Sydney Porter – better-known by his pen name, O. Henry – was born in Greensboro, USA in 1862. In his youth, he was an avid reader, but left school at the age of fifteen to work on a Texas ranch. Some years later, Porter moved to Austin, where in 1884 he started a humorous weekly *The Rolling Stone*. When this venture failed, he joined the *Houston Post* as a reporter – however, his work was cut short when, in 1898, he was sent to jail for a still-debated embezzlement conviction.

Porter started writing short stories while in prison, in order to support his family on the outside. His first work, 'Whistling Dick's Christmas Stocking' (1899), appeared in *McClure's Magazine*. Upon emerging from incarceration in 1901, Porter changed his name to O. Henry, and began writing in earnest.

Henry moved to New York City in 1902, and for the next few years produced a story a week for the *New York World*. His first collection, *Cabbages and Kings*, appeared in 1904, and was followed two years later by his *The Four Million*. This latter collection included his well-known stories 'The Gift of the Magi' and 'The Furnished Room'. Henry's best-known piece is the much-anthologized 'The Ransom of the Red Chief', which appeared in his 1910 collection *Whirligigs*.

Over the course of his life, he produced a total of ten books, and more than 600 short stories.

In later life, Henry was blighted by alcoholism, ill health and debt. He died of cirrhosis of the liver in 1910, aged 47, and three more of his collections – *Sixes And Sevens* (1911), *Rolling Stones* (1912) and *Waifs And Strays* (1917) – appeared posthumously.Nowadays, Henry is regarded as a master of the short form, and an innovator of the 'twist' ending.The O. Henry Award, named in his memory, is now a highly prestigious annual prize.

ERNEST HAYCOX

Ernest James Haycox was born in Portland, Oregon in 1899. He enlisted in the United States Army in 1915 and spent World War I in Europe. At the end of the war, he returned home and enrolled at the University of Oregon, graduating in 1923 with a degree in journalism. Following a short stint with *The Oregonian* in Portland as a police-beat reporter, Haycox spent the next two years living in New York City, and it was here – where he developed a deep interest in the American Revolution, which would then spawn his love of Western fiction – that he began to write.

By the thirties, Haycox was a regular contributor to *Collier's Weekly*. Most of his work was imaginative Western adventure but, around the mid-thirties, perhaps beginning with his 1935 'Trouble Shooter' (which went on to become the film *Union Pacific*), his stories adopted more of a factual, historic air. By the end of his career, Haycox had published 14 novels and nearly 100 short stories with *Collier's* — a record for the publication. In 1943 he also started to publish in *The Saturday Evening Post*. Haycox had a large and dedicated readership – amongst others, Ernest Hemingway stated that "I read *The Saturday Evening Post* whenever it has a serial by Ernest Haycox."

Haycox also had some success in Hollywood. Most

notably, his short story 'Stage to Lordsburg', published in 1937, was adapted into the movie *Stagecoach*, directed by John Ford and starring John Wayne in the role that made him an icon. After briefly dabbling with a career in politics – a major public figure, he declared openly his belief that the US should enter the war against Nazi Germany and, from 1944 onwards, warned repeatedly against renewed isolationism – Haycox died at his home in Oregon, several months after unsuccessful cancer surgery.

MAX BRAND

Frederick Schiller Faust — perhaps better-known by his many pen names, one of which is 'Max Brand' — was born in Seatde, USA in 1892. He grew up in California, and attended the University of California in Berkeley, but left before graduating due to bad behaviour.In 1915, Faust joined the Canadian Army, but deserted after a year and went to New York City.

During the 1910s, Faust wrote prolifically, and began to sell stories to pulp magazines such as *All-Story Weekly* and *Argosy Magazine*. This continued into the twenties; at one point, he was writing more than a million words a year for *Western Story Magazine*. As it turned out, it was within the Western genre that Faust became both best-known and best-respected.His works, by the standards of most such tales, were highly thoughtful and literary.

Beginning in 1934, Faust began to publish fiction in upscale literary magazines that paid better than pulps.A few years later he became a screenwriter in Hollywood, where he eventually went on to earn around $3,000 a week, making him one of the highestpaid writers of his era. However,Faust himself disparaged his commercial success, and only used his real name for his poetry — the one section of his oeuvre he considered to be truly literary.

During World War II, Faust worked as a frontline war correspondent.In 1944, while travelling with American soldiers in Italy in, he was mortally wounded by shrapnel. He died aged 51.

ZANE GREY

Pearl Zane Gray was born in Zanesville, Ohio (a town founded by his maternal ancestor Ebenezer Zane) in 1872. As well as being a keen reader of adventure stories and dime novels, Grey was a talented young baseball player, and won a scholarship to the University of Pennsylvania, from where he graduated with a degree in dentistry in 1898. Shortly before turning thirty, Grey moved to New York to set up his first dental clinic. He often left the city to go fishing and camping, and it was in 1900, while canoeing in the upper Delaware River, that he met Dolly, his future wife. The couple married in 1905, and when Dolly inherited a large sum of money, Grey was able to cease his dental practice and turn full-time to his nascent literary pursuits.

Dolly managed her husband's finances and contract negotiations – and tolerated his many infidelities – while Grey wrote, and the two of them split his income down the middle. His first magazine article, 'A Day on the Delaware', had been published in the May 1902 issue of *Recreation* magazine, but Grey found himself increasingly turning to Western fiction, having read Owen Wister's novel *The Virginian*. He struggled at first, even self-publishing his first work, *Betty Zane*. He followed this with its more successful sequel, *Spirit of the Border* (1906), his Grand Canyon inspired novel *The Last of the Plainsmen* (1908), *The Last Trail* (1909) and his first bonafide best-seller, *The Heritage of the Desert* (1910). But real success came in 1912, with *Riders of the Purple Sage*, Grey's best-known and most acclaimed novel, and one of the most popular works of Western fiction of all time.

Due to the financial success of *Riders of the Purple Sage*, Grey had the time and money to engage in his first and greatest passion: fishing. From 1918 until 1932, he was a regular contributor to *Outdoor Life* magazine, and as one of its celebrity writers did much to popularize big-game fishing. He continued to write prolifically in short bursts of inspiration for the rest of his life, and remained hugely popular; indeed, he became one of the first millionaire authors, and his total book sales now exceed 40 million. From 1925 to his death, he travelled a number of unspoiled lands, particularly the islands of South Pacific, New Zealand and Australia. Grey died in his home in Altadena, California, in 1939. Since his death, 110 films have been made that are based on his work.